KU-183-895

Award-winning author Anthony Masters knows how 'to hook his reader from the first page' Books for Keeps. He wrote extensively for young adults and was renowned for tackling serious issues through gripping stories. He has also written for adults, both fiction and non-fiction. For the Orchard Black Apple list he wrote several books including *The Drop*, *Day of the Dead*, shortlisted for the Angus Book Award and *Wicked*. Sadly, Anthony Masters died suddenly in April 2003. His presence will be keenly missed in the world of children's books.

Rave reviews for *The Drop*:

'An intense psychological study.'
Times Educational Supplement

'A plot which moves along a such a lick is likely to keep readers engaged right up to the dramatic finale.'
Books for Keeps

WS 2245854 9

CR
F
MAS

ALSO BY ANTHONY MASTERS

BLACK APPLES

Day of the Dead
Web of Terror
Wicked

RED APPLES

Shark Attack
Hunted
Bear Trap
Killer instinct

THE DROP

ANTHONY MASTERS

ORCHARD BOOKS

To Megan Larkin - an inspirational and meticulous editor.

ORCHARD BOOKS
96 Leonard Street, London EC2A 4XD
Orchard Books Australia
32/45-51 Huntley Street, Alexandria, NSW 2015
ISBN 1 84362 196 7
A paperback original
First published in Great Britain in 2000
This edition published in 2004
Text © Anthony Masters 2000
The right of Anthony Masters to be identified as the author of this
work has been asserted by him in accordance with the
Copyright, Designs and Patents Act, 1988.
A CIP catalogue record for this book is available from the British Library.
1 3 5 7 9 10 8 6 4 2
Printed in Great Britain
www.wattspub.co.uk

Sean Dexter was hanging upside down, legs strapped to a beam. His tied hands rested on the toilet seat, taking the full weight of his body. A message had been scrawled across his forehead in black felt-tipped pen and Sean knew what it was. The same words had been written across Tim's, only a fortnight ago. I'VE BEEN DROPPED.

Looking down into the scummy, stinking toilet, Sean wondered how long his punishment would last. Of course, he knew who was behind it all, but he wouldn't dare to grass. There was something about Oliver that terrified him. Oliver was weird. Oliver was mad.

Checking his watch, Sean saw he had been suspended for almost half an hour, although it felt much longer, and, apart from the blood that had run to his head, making his temples pound, he felt sick and his wrists were hurting badly.

Oliver's physical strength had been a surprise. Sean had fought with fists and head and feet, but Oliver was stronger. The other four would definitely have been able to restrain him, but Sean had to admit that Oliver alone was more than enough. Didn't madmen have enormous strength – and cunning?

Or was he making it all up to save his own face? The blood pounding in his temples was making him increasingly dizzy and it was hard to think logically at all. He kicked out with his legs

5

yet again, but the rope that was tied round his ankles was too tight. Anyway, if he did break free Sean knew he would fall like a stone and probably crack his head open. He'd just have to wait for rescue — if it ever came. Tim had been hanging upside down for ages before the caretaker had found him.

Sean was even more terrified of the gag in his mouth, a large dirty handkerchief that threatened to choke him. Suppose he was sick. Would he be suffocated by his own vomit?

Meanwhile, the insect life in the abandoned toilet was readjusting to the upside-down figure of the fourteen-year-old intruder. When Sean had been strung up, still struggling, the spiders, beetles and woodlice had retreated to their lairs, but now, to his disgust, they were gradually, relentlessly returning. A vast web, thick with dead flies, shook slightly under the toilet as its dark occupant stirred. A black beetle scuttled across the dusty floor and woodlice dropped from the battered door frame, joining the beetle in its journey of discovery. Sean had always had a creeping horror of insects. Now he was surrounded by them.

ONE

Greg trudged past the abandoned toilet block, anxious to kill time. He'd been at St Peter's, Wandsworth, for two weeks of the summer term, and still hadn't made any friends. As a result, free time seemed to last for an eternity. As usual, he had eaten lunch alone in the canteen, self-consciously trying to select a table where someone else might be alone, but finding only crowds of friends, laughing and joking, shutting him out.

All the other students had been together for a couple of years, and he had known he'd be an outsider from the start – but not *this* much of an outsider. His loneliness hurt badly.

So, in spare moments that seemed to stretch into eternity, he read his favourite series of fantasy novels – *Dream Stealer* – and no wonder he was already up to number five. As he read, however, Greg wondered desperately how long his isolation would last.

The Parkers had moved to Wandsworth from Dorset and Greg, athletic, well built and good looking with his swept-back fair hair and clear complexion, had been happy at the school in Swanage where he had had plenty of friends and had never felt lonely at all. Last summer he had sailed, canoed and played cricket on a village green. Here, where everything was urban and unfamiliar, he felt trapped. Even the Parkers' large Victorian home seemed shabby and tawdry, the unkempt garden a wilderness, the pavement outside dog-stained and litter-strewn, the shopping mall packed with crowds of alien teenagers, undermining his confidence by their remoteness, as if he was invisible.

Yes – that was exactly how he felt, thought Greg. He was the invisible boy. His parents obviously didn't feel like that at all. Dad loved his new job in London, Mum had taken to her secretarial job at the clinic like a 'duck to water' and was already on chatting terms with the neighbours. But the neighbours only had young children and there was no one his age at all. Worse still, just as they had put the Dorset house on the market, Dad had excitedly told Greg that Mum was going to have a baby.

He had immediately felt betrayed and since they had arrived in Wandsworth his parents seemed as remote and as cut-off as everyone else. Although Greg had known they were unhappy and not getting on, that they wanted a 'fresh start', he had tried to arm himself against the change. But now it had come he felt worse than he ever thought he could, and his mother had delivered the final blow by giving birth to Rachel - another stranger to shut him out, to make him invisible.

The broken-down door of the toilets was swinging open in the bright May sunshine and Greg smelt a sour, shut-in smell which seemed to represent everything he disliked about London, and Wandsworth in particular.

Then he thought he heard a noise – a kind of mumbling sound. Weren't these toilets where the smokers went? If so, he'd better move on. Greg didn't like smokers – or smoking. His father smoked at least fifty a day, and the new house already smelt acrid. He couldn't remember the Dorset house smelling like that. But then 95 Larchfield Gardens, Swanage, had already become sanctified in Greg's mind, for nowhere could be as heartbreakingly homely. The sense of loss engulfed him again and he swallowed hard, aware of the tears at the back of his eyes, desperate for them not to fall, for if they did they would go on falling for a very long time – as they did at night. Every night.

The mumbling sound came again, but this time it was like a desperate grunt. Greg paused and then cautiously went inside.

He backed away, staring up incredulously at the nightmare figure. Dangling by his ankles, strapped to a beam, the boy's face was a kind of reddish black, and as he began to thump his tied hands on the filthy toilet seat, the grunting became a coughing howl.

'OK,' whispered Greg. 'OK.' But he didn't move, and the muffled grunting became even louder while the boy's hands thumped the toilet seat so viciously that some of the plastic broke away in little shards. 'OK.' Greg finally stumbled into the stifling space. It didn't take long to untie the boy's hands, but Greg wasn't tall enough to reach the beam. Then he realised he would be if he stood on the toilet seat.

Clumsily, almost overbalancing, Greg clambered up and began to try to untie the cord that held the boy's ankles. After a long struggle it suddenly slackened and they both fell, Sean doing a back-flip, almost kicking Greg in the face. They tumbled into a heap in the corner, rolling clear of each other, sitting up and then getting shakily to their feet.

Sean tugged at the gag around his mouth and eventually managed to pull it away. His face was still a strange muddy red colour, slowly turning to a chalky white as he leant against the wall.

Now Greg could read the message on his forehead.

'What does that –' he began, but Sean waved him away.

'I'm going to be sick.' He bent over and vomited on to the floor, the smell overpowering, and Greg began to gag. Desperate to get away from the stench, he stumbled outside, breathing in fresh air, wondering if he was going to be sick himself.

A few seconds later, Sean, his eyes full of tears and strands of vomit clinging to his face and clothes, followed Greg outside, throwing himself down on the grass and lying there, breathing heavily, his eyes closed, chest heaving.

'I'll get someone,' said Greg weakly.

'They might come back.'

'Who?'

'The Geeks. It doesn't matter. They won't – they can't put me through it again.'

'Who are you on about? Who are these Geeks?' demanded Greg.

'They're a creepy bunch of nerds,' gasped Sean. 'They grabbed me and I got dragged down to the old toilet block. They're led by this weird guy.'

'What's his name?'

'Oliver Cole. He's crazy.'

'In what way?'

'He says Adam Anlott's his dad.'

'The author of *Dream Stealer*?' asked Greg in amazement.

'I mean,' said Sean with feeling, 'how *could* Adam Anlott be Oliver's father? They don't even have the same name. Anyway, *Oliver* couldn't have anyone famous as a dad. He's too much of a prat, too much of a weirdo and a nutter and a geek.'

'Is that so?' asked Greg.

'Go and get some help then,' snarled Sean. 'I don't feel well.'

If it hadn't been for me, thought Greg, you might have felt a whole lot worse. Surely some thanks were due? He began to run towards the school buildings, the stench of vomit still strong in his nostrils. Nevertheless, he kept wondering about Adam Anlott. Was it a pseudonym? Suppose Anlott really was Oliver's father. That would be a bit of a turn up for the books!

Then Greg turned back. 'What's your name?'

'Sean Dexter.' The boy paused, adding almost grudgingly, 'Thanks.' Then he was sick all over the grass.

Oliver sat in class, staring ahead, wondering how Sean was getting on, thinking about making an excuse so that he could run down to the old toilets and release him. He had almost done the same for Tim a fortnight ago. But in the end he hadn't, although he had been very scared, amazed at what he had eventually been capable of doing. Of course his hatred had driven him on, but Oliver was still surprised how hard he could hate. It seemed to have happened so quickly.

Not so long ago, Oliver would never have condoned such violence. 'I never knew he had it in him,' he had overheard Pug telling the other Geeks. Oliver had never known he had it in him either. One moment he was playing at zapping an alien invasion in one of his computer games. The next moment he was zapping Sweats for real. One moment he would never have got physical with anyone. The next he was wrestling Sean to the ground outside the old toilet block in readiness for the Geeks to string him up.

I'M SURPRISED BY MYSELF, Oliver wrote in capital letters on the inside cover of his homework diary. Then he wrote it again. I'M SURPRISED BY MYSELF. Then he scribbled it all out.

Tonight he would sit in his room and look out at the tree.

Tonight he would talk to Mum and explain to her why he had come to do what he did. He wrote again in his homework diary. A MAN'S GOT TO DO WHAT A MAN'S GOT TO DO. He looked down. The statement was good. Mum would understand, but of course Oliver also knew that she wouldn't.

It's not fair, he thought childishly, wanting her back, wanting Mum to stop this man doing what this man's got to do. Anyway, he wasn't a man and it wasn't his fault. The Sweats had gone too far. They'd been going too far for a long time, picking on him like that.

Sean had thrown his briefcase in the swimming pool and ruined all his school books. Tim had punched him in the face and made his nose bleed. And Ryan – Ryan had committed the worst crime of all against him. Ryan had taken the last present his mother had ever given him, just before she died. Ryan had taken the jade pendant she had always worn, torn it off the leather thong that Oliver had hung round his own neck, and chucked it down the toilet, pulling the chain. Oliver had never recovered the pendant and that's why the Sweats were taking the Drop. Soon Ryan would take a bigger one.

The other Geeks had been bullied too. They had been beaten up and had lost personal possessions and been publicly humiliated, so it had been easy to lead them into retaliation. All roads led to the Drop, thought Oliver. All roads.

TWO

Greg sat on the end of a line of chairs in the assembly hall. After leaving Sean Dexter, he had run to the office and told the secretary what he had found. The bell had rung and Greg had been briskly told to go into lessons – an instruction he had bitterly resented. Wasn't anyone going to thank him properly? In Swanage he was sure he would have been a hero. In Wandsworth, he was nothing. He still felt appalled by what had happened. Did this school have boys hanging from their ankles over dirty toilets every day of the week? Greg hadn't been to an all-boys school before and its narrowness already seemed to hem him in. Boys confined to their own unalleviated company were competitive and aggressive. There were too many underdogs.

Mr James, the head teacher, was standing on the platform alone, resting his hands on the lectern, while the teachers sat in serried ranks in the aisles of the hall. He looked devastated and spoke slowly, weighing every word.

'I don't think I've ever been so shaken in the whole of my career as a teacher.'

The students of St Peter's School leant forward with a mixture of curiosity and heady anticipation.

'First Tim Rathbone and now Sean Dexter. It's barbaric,

and when I find out who is responsible – and I already have a strong suspicion who *is* responsible – they'll be severely punished.' Mr James cleared his throat. 'Sean, like Tim, was found hanging upside down in the old toilet block. His feet were tied to a beam and his hands were resting on the seat.'

Someone gave a slightly hysterical giggle which was taken up by a few other boys.

'It's not funny.' Mr James was contemptuous and the laughter died guiltily away. 'It's not funny at all. Those boys who just found Sean's predicament funny have been noted.'

Some teachers sitting in the aisles nodded as they stared threateningly at the culprits.

'Sean could have died.' Mr James's voice was full of quiet authority. 'So could Tim.' Then he began to speak more rapidly. 'Over the first few weeks of this summer term I've had cause to suspend certain boys in Year Nine – boys who have recently been given permission to return – but the situation has run out of control again, and I shall, of course, be carrying out a full investigation. Meanwhile, Sean, like Tim, has been taken to casualty for a check-up. I must stress to you all that I'm taking this assault extremely seriously and, in consultation with both boys' parents, I may well be talking to the police who will regard the incidents equally seriously. They may even press charges.'

Mr James paused again and the silence in the hall deepened.

'As you all know, in the first case, our caretaker

fortunately discovered Tim who had been hanging upside down in the toilets for some time. Sean had also been hanging for nearly half an hour when he was discovered by a student who, with considerable initiative, helped Sean down and immediately went for help. That boy is Greg Parker.' Mr James paused again. 'Greg has only recently moved to St Peter's from a school in Dorset. Heaven knows what he must think of us. Is this the sort of example of a London school that we want to give Greg? A place of violence? Of gang warfare? St Peter's was never like that. But how is Greg to know?'

Greg squirmed, knowing all the eyes in the assembly hall were trying to search him out. But eventually they gave up. He was, after all, invisible.

Oliver Cole sat on the edge of the abandoned roller-skating rink. He was tall, gawky, with a shock of black hair that had been tied into a pigtail. As he lay back against the rusty iron pillar, Oliver gazed at the debris around him, noticing that some of the ceiling tiles had fallen into the rink and an old Coca Cola vending machine had been pushed through the glassless window of the skate store, while the small rink-side cafe was a jumble of upended chairs and tables.

The Geeks had been vandalising the place in his absence, but what did he care? He liked the mess.

Oliver watched over his domain with pleasure and pride. No one came here, with the exception of an old vagrant called Molly who the Geeks had successfully scared away – but only after a considerable verbal battle. 'This is my home,' Molly had yelled, retreating in slow defeat, pushing away her supermarket trolley, loaded with carrier bags containing all her worldly possessions.

'It isn't any more,' Oliver had told her.

'You lot are up to no good,' she had muttered. 'What do you want with a place like this?'

Waiting for his companions to arrive, Oliver felt a sense of triumph. Tim and Sean had taken the Drop. But Ryan would get something bigger than that.

Oliver often thought about Ryan. In fact he was in his mind all the time. Ryan, Oliver considered, was afraid of anyone who was different, just like Tim and Sean were. They all three wanted to look the same, be the same, do the same. They were into sport, into being heroes. But they were also violent bullies. Ryan's group had become known as the Sweats.

Pug, Denny, Hassan and Fabian were exactly the reverse, and under Oliver's leadership they wanted to be as different as possible. Although St Peter's students wore a compulsory uniform, the Geeks had added certain individual touches to their appearance. Oliver had his pigtail, Pug's hair was so short that it was virtually stubble, Hassan wore dreadlocks, Denny's hair was lavishly gelled and Fabian, almost as wide as he was tall, had beaded dreadlocks. The head, while sticking rigorously to the uniform rule, allowed this expression of individuality for all his pupils. He didn't want to be seen as old-fashioned – or so Oliver supposed.

Oliver got up and began to walk around the abandoned rink, lord of all he surveyed. The Geeks had come together *because* they were different. In an all-boys school, the pecking order was rigid. There were the cool and laid-back brigade, all of whom were into sport. There were the boffins who were computer-obsessed. There were the high fliers, who were in the top sets and heading for Oxford or Cambridge, an elitist group who kept to themselves. Then there were the shy, and the lonely and retiring. At the bottom of the heap, in the shadows, were the Geeks.

Some months ago, the Sweats had decided to pick on them.

In Oliver's opinion, the campaign was a typically crude response to one of his assertions of individuality. Compelled by Mr James to watch an important school match, he and Pug had turned their backs on the action, unseen by staff but spotted by Ryan who was the captain of St Peter's Under Fifteens. The school had lost. Humiliated by defeat, Ryan had begun his campaign against the Geeks and he, Tim and Sean, as well as other boys they had casually drawn in, were systematic and unsparing. The Geeks had suffered badly and there seemed no possibility of the campaign ending until Oliver had discovered that the Sweats were forcing sponsorship for a football tournament from some of the richer boys in the school – and that the reluctant subscribers were prepared to grass, providing they were promised protection.

Oliver had gone to his head of year with the dilemma. She had gone to the head teacher, and Mr James's retribution had been swift. As chief culprits, Ryan, Tim and Sean had been suspended and publicly disgraced. They had returned to school chastened and ashamed. But Oliver had promised the Geeks that this was only the beginning. Authority had prevailed, but guerilla warfare would take a greater toll.

Oliver now hated the Sweats with paranoic intensity, for they had made him a victim and he couldn't bear that, for he was a victim already. The jade pendant had been lost for ever. He would never forgive Ryan for that.

'It's a simple case of bullying,' his dad had said to him. 'You've got to learn to toughen up.' And he had. Once Oliver had read in one of his mother's poetry books,

This is the law of the Yukon,
that only the Strong shall thrive,
That surely the Weak shall perish
and only the Fit survive.

Well, he could get himself fit, couldn't he? *It's a simple case of bullying. You've got to learn to toughen up.*

I'll toughen up for you, Mum. When you weren't dead, I wasn't like this. But now you *are*, I'll remember the law of the Yukon. If I'm weak, I'll perish. If I'm fit, I'll survive.

So the Sweats will take the Drop, one by one. And Ryan will take the greatest Drop of all.

Oliver strolled up the steps beside the spectators' gallery and opened a door on to the remains of a gym, with rusty steel bars, a rowing machine and an exercise bike.

He mounted the rowing machine, and the ancient equipment began to squeak and protest as he pulled himself to and fro. He had to make himself even fitter and stronger. Originally light-boned and weedy, despite his height, Oliver was developing solid muscle and his confidence was soaring.

As he exercised, Oliver noticed he was no longer gasping for breath, no longer aching all over. Instead, his strokes were strong and powerful. He saw Ryan's handsome, square-jawed face with its clear complexion, his close-cropped hair and stocky shoulders. One day I'll kill you, Oliver promised himself, as beads of sweat gathered on his brow.

Oliver got off the rowing machine and pushed open the creaking door that was half off its hinges. The next area had once been a badminton court but now held a make-shift assault course. Here, Oliver and the Geeks had developed even more stamina and agility in preparation for their war against the Sweats. The result was exhilarating and almost miraculous, for none of them had taken much interest in body-building before.

Oliver contemplated the course, constructed from ropes

stolen from a construction site, wood from the old rink and a pulley 'found' in the gym store at school. Out of these basic materials the Geeks had made a high rope-walk, a death slide, a climbing wall, a rope ladder and a swing.

Oliver looked up at the high ropes and shuddered. They were the reason he had come to the rink early, for this was the only piece of equipment he hadn't dared try, despite the fact that the others had tackled the course countless times.

Oliver suffered from vertigo and had done his best to avoid the ropes, succeeding until his lieutenant, Pug, short and round-shouldered with a broken nose and a baby face, had pointed out his oversight. 'You haven't been over yet, Ollie,' he had complained. *'We've* all had to do it. Why not you?'

'I will next time,' Oliver had replied.

Pug had stared at him hard and then turned away.

Oliver had known immediately what the stare had been about. Pug was his rival. Pug wanted to take over the leadership of the Geeks. Pug was always putting Oliver down behind his back, saying he was a dreamer and that he never intended to do anything to the Sweats at all. But Oliver was determined to stay leader, to convince Pug and the others that he could do anything they could do – and do it much better!

So now here Oliver was, gazing up at the high ropes apprehensively.

To put off the dreadful experience for a few more precious seconds, Oliver opened the door into what had once been a weight-training room. Here, another amateur conversion had been made, but this time the construction was more ambitious.

Some months ago, Oliver had discovered a pile of three-metre poles in the basement of the rink, which he thought must originally have been intended for some kind of adventure playground that had never been built. The Geeks had lugged the poles up the stairs, setting them upright and securing them with lashed ropes. They had then created a shaky platform from sheets of board, taken surreptitiously from Denny's father's builders yard, by banging nails through them into the top of each pole. On the platform a post had been secured, from which hung a thick rope, and a hook had been bolted into the underside of the platform.

Oliver looked at the contraption with singular satisfaction. Then, slowly and hesitantly, he returned to the assault course and to the horror of the high ropes.

Oliver gazed up, remembering how he had first grassed the Sweats to his head of year, Marian Stokes. It was a particularly fond memory, and a slow smile of satisfaction spread over Oliver's face.

'I can prove it,' he had told an uneasy Mrs Stokes, who was all too clearly trying not to believe him. 'I've got witnesses.'

'Who?' she had asked suspiciously.

'Terry Briggs and Chris Summers.'

'They'll come and see me, will they?'

'They're waiting outside the door, miss.'

'I see.' She looked even more uneasy. Marian Stokes had always thought well of the Sweats and knew nothing of their bullying ways. 'I find all this very hard to accept, Oliver.'

'You *will*, miss, when you hear what Terry and Chris have got to say. But you've got to promise to protect them, miss. If you don't, they won't talk.'

'You make it sound as if this school's being run by the Mafia, Oliver.'

'It is a bit like that,' he had begun, but Mrs Stokes wouldn't listen to any more. She had listened to Terry and Chris, however, gradually becoming convinced they were telling the truth. Ryan, Sean and Tim were then interviewed by the head and suspended.

Oliver's triumph, however, had been somewhat dampened when Ryan had walked casually across to him in the school playground on the day he returned.

'You grassed us.'

'I didn't.'

'Don't bother to argue.' Ryan had looked at Oliver with the same focus of hatred as Oliver had for Ryan – but he had still been surprised by its ferocity. 'You're a freak,' Ryan had continued. 'What are you?'

Oliver had remained silent.

'You're a freak.' Ryan had tapped him on the chest. 'Only a freak would say his father was Adam Anlott.'

'He *is* my father.'

'Prove it,' Ryan had urged.

'How?'

'Ask him to come into school.'

'My father doesn't like schools.'

'Ask me over to your place. I'd like to meet the guy.'

'He wouldn't want to meet you.'

Ryan poked him in the chest again. 'You're a bullshitter,' he had said. Then he had walked away.

Slowly, Oliver moved towards the rope ladder. Step by step he began to climb. Ryan's words had hurt him badly and he would have to be made to pay.

THREE

Oliver reached up for the top rope. He had got this far before but had not been able to move, remaining frozen on the ladder. This time, however, the surge of adrenalin, the certainty of Ryan's fate and the increasing confidence in himself made Oliver gingerly step on to the lower rope and begin to edge along. As he did so, step by staggering step, he remembered Ryan saying over and over again, 'What are you? You're a freak. What are you? You're a freak.' Then he saw him flushing the pendant down the toilet – over and over and over again.

Suddenly, Oliver's confidence waned, and as the rope bridge began to sway he came to an abrupt halt. Looking down, knees trembling, wrists weakening, he shut his eyes against the vertigo, mentally glimpsing his father at the typewriter in his study upstairs, the old green card-table shaking. He knocked on the door.

Dad?
What do you want?
It's lunch time.
Bring it up. I can't stop.
I need to talk to you.
Tonight.

You're going out tonight.

For God's sake. Tomorrow, then. What the hell — just leave me alone.

What the hell, thought Oliver as the rope bridge steadied again. He had to be stronger – stronger than even his fellow Geeks. After all, they might be his enemies too, one day; he was always aware that Pug was trying to undermine him, but the others seemed happy enough, enjoying the strange atmosphere of the old rink, content to have a good laugh, swap horror books and generally muck around. I've got to be strong enough to keep them, thought Oliver, as he took more hesitant steps across the bridge, which began to sway again. He froze, trying to dredge up more inner resources to keep him going, to reach the other side without looking down. If he *did* look down, he might fall – plunging to the concrete below, smashing his skull like an egg-shell.

Oliver shut his eyes, desperately trying to focus. He *must* prove himself. The Geeks must never question his leadership again.

Sudden exhilaration filled Oliver as he came to the middle of the high ropes, and he no longer had the all too familiar drawing feeling – as if the floor below was rushing up, a torrent of air that would claw at his feet and eventually bring him down, head over heels.

A feeling of heady triumph swept Oliver as he began to

climb towards the sanctuary of the ladder on the far side. He was going to make it – for the first time ever. Determinedly, he refused to think of the drop beneath him, fixing his mind on the pain of his mother's death.

She had been dead for two years, yet it still seemed only yesterday she had taken Oliver in her wasted arms and kissed him goodbye and given him the pendant to hang round his neck. A few hours later she was dead from an inoperable cancer.

The drawing feeling returned, but Oliver refused to allow himself to look down. He closed his eyes again.

When his mother had been alive, he had never needed to know Dad. Now she was like a barrier between them as they lived their separate lives in the empty house. Although Oliver understood that his father was still grieving deeply, there was no way he could reach him. Dad had retreated into his writing, shutting himself away, rarely emerging, and although Oliver tried to look after him, cooking meals and cleaning the house, his efforts only seemed to make his father resent him even more.

Sometimes his grandparents came and stayed, or Oliver would visit them at their house in Kingston. When this happened, he was almost happy again, but the stay never lasted long enough.

'Mum,' he gasped involuntarily as he reached the ladder, and then thanked God no one was around to hear him sounding so stupid.

★

Oliver scrambled down the rope ladder, feeling both elation and grief, immediately replacing one fear with another. Would he *ever* get through to his father?

Everything else seemed easy. Grassing the Sweats, even clambering over the high ropes, the future certainty of getting Ryan – it was all simple compared with reaching his father.

Then Oliver remembered his faint ray of hope when Dad had said carelessly a few weeks ago, 'One day, why don't we write a *Dream Stealer* together? A father and son job.' Oliver knew his dad had been drinking, but he painfully thrust the knowledge away.

For the last few weeks, Oliver had been outlining just such an idea – a plot for *Dream Stealer* – and he was almost ready to present it to his father. But he kept hanging back, fearing rejection, and, worse still, ridicule.

Oliver glanced at his watch. He had ten minutes before the others arrived so he would be able to go over the plot again. Let Dad like it, Oliver prayed. Please let him like my *Dream Stealer*.

Greg was bursting to tell his parents all about his dramatic rescue of Sean and the official praise he had received. Several boys from his tutor group had come up to him, muttering congratulations, but they soon drifted away, and Greg was alone again.

Dad and Mum were home, upstairs with the baby, and once again Greg felt the yawning isolation as he heard Rachel crying and the murmuring sound of his parents trying to comfort her.

He slammed the front door and Rachel began to cry louder. Heading for the kitchen, Greg heard feet on the stairs. Now I'm in trouble, he thought miserably, but instead he heard his father shouting, 'Home is the hero!'

Greg looked up, bewildered, to see Dad running towards him in delight, his eyes alive with excitement, grabbing his waist and swinging him round.

Then Dad let him go, gasping and out of breath but still managing to clap Greg on the back until it hurt.

'What are you on about?'

'I'm on about you and how you rescued this boy. Sean something.'

'How do you know?'

'The head phoned. He was over the moon. Said you'd done a power of good for the morale of St Peter's at a difficult time – and you've only been there five minutes.'

'Half a term.' Greg was bewildered by the fuss, partly pleased, partly wanting to find something wrong. 'Where's Mum?' he asked abruptly.

'Feeding Rachel. She won't be long.'

She'd be down here now if she loved me, thought Greg.

Meanwhile, Dad was babbling on. 'Of course, we never wanted you to go to an all-boys' school. But St Peter's has got the best academic record in the area so –' He paused and then rushed on. 'I know how much you miss Swanage. I mean, we all do. But this promotion has given me a lot more money and we'll be able to take some great holidays –' The baby began to scream upstairs. 'And Rachel's a bit of a fresh start for us all, isn't she?'

Greg couldn't imagine for one moment why she should be, and merely scowled.

His father looked uneasy and Greg wondered if he had guessed how he had been feeling. But he couldn't admit to being jealous of his baby sister, and even if Dad had raised the subject he knew he wouldn't have confessed.

'Well,' said his father a little wildly. 'Let's all have a nice cup of tea.' He always said that when he couldn't think of anything else to say and normally Greg loved him for the flat little expression, but now he merely felt irritated.

Oliver returned to the edge of the rink and sat down again, pulling out a copy of his father's latest book from under a rusty metal chair. He stared down at the garishly mystical cover which read: *DREAM STEALER 6: The Haunting of Doug Johnson.*

The series was becoming increasingly popular, a cult that was taking on thousands of readers. Before *Dream Stealer*, Dad had only written pot-boiling thrillers which had never sold in any great numbers and made very little money. But then, of course, Mum had been alive and she had had a well-paid job in marketing. She had always been the bread-winner and it was not until she had died that Dad had been advised to try the teenage series. Now the publishers wanted more and more *Dream Stealers*, so there was an official reason as well as an unofficial one for Dad keeping his head down.

The books were about a contemporary magician, quietly living in Penge with his shrewish wife. During the day he was a conventional bank manager, but at night Peter Pendall wandered abroad, stealing people's dreams and sometimes using them against the dreamer or for some wider, deadlier purpose.

In the current book, the *Dream Stealer* had stolen the dream of a young girl who hated her bullying stepmother and fantasised about her death. Peter Pendall then placed the dream in the stepmother's mind. Oliver read on, exhilarated as usual by his father's clear, terse, undemanding prose.

She woke, shuddering. Anna Hardcastle had never had the imagination to dream as vividly as this before and she was deeply shocked by what she had dreamt.

Her stepdaughter, Kathy, had picked up the long, sharp meat knife and advanced towards her that Christmas morning. The air was full of the smell of roasting turkey. Soon it could be full of the smell of stuck pig. The knife in Kathy's hand was only inches from Anna's throat when she suddenly woke.

Oliver stopped reading, more interested in what he was writing himself. He also began to fantasise, imagining his father's reaction to the first few paragraphs. 'Ollie – this is terrific stuff. Do you really want to work with your old Dad? I mean – you could turn out to be the better writer...' Slowly, but without much difficulty, the idea had been born.

DREAM STEALER 7
Taking the Drop

Ryan Banks woke up screaming. He had dreamt what fate had in store for him. As his head was thrust into the noose he began to beg for mercy. But there could be no mercy, for the Stealer had reached into his unconscious mind and made his dream the grimmest reality of his pathetic life.

Oliver was interrupted by a crashing sound as Pug arrived, slamming the door of the old rink so hard it rattled on its hinges.

'Shut up,' Oliver hissed.

'There's no one around,' Pug said casually, as if he wasn't interested in what Oliver felt at all.

Oliver felt Pug's threat again. A highly intelligent petty thief, Oliver sensed that Pug would much rather lead the Geeks into shoplifting than take revenge on Ryan. Because of this, Oliver had made the Geeks a false promise. He had told them that if they got Tim and Sean and Ryan – especially Ryan – they could expect to be rewarded. Now the Geeks had fulfilled two-thirds of the plan, they would soon expect that reward. But Oliver only thought of the immediate future.

'We don't want anyone to know we're here,' said Oliver, trying to assert his authority.

'They won't.' Pug sat down beside him. The old rink was behind an equally abandoned pub on a dual carriageway that had been bypassed a couple of years ago. 'What are you writing?'

'Nothing.' Oliver hastily crammed his notebook into the back pocket of his jeans.

He never invited any of his fellow Geeks home. No one had ever believed his father was Adam Anlott and Oliver saw no point in trying to convince them now. But in spite of their mutual distrust, Pug and Oliver put up with each other. They were both natural conspirators; the planning that had gone into 'dropping' both Tim and Sean had been intricate.

'What's new?'

'I think we should get Ryan sooner rather than later.' Oliver spoke with confidence and conviction.

'Why?'

'The others will soon get fed up. They want more out of the Geeks than – what they're getting. Don't you agree?'

They both risked eye contact, remembering Oliver's

promise and Pug's wider ambitions. Pug and his mother lived in real poverty, entirely dependent on state benefit. He needed money and much the same could be said of the other Geeks.

In his worst moments, Oliver wondered why he had been able to exert any authority over them at all. He was good with words, he supposed, and then there was the fact that in needing to improve his own physique he had also improved theirs. It was he who had designed the assault course. But Oliver still knew his leadership was built on shifting sands. The Geeks thought he would eventually offer them something big, something worth having. They hadn't a clue what that might be. Neither did Oliver. But they believed in him. The Geeks were a mixed bag, not all thieves like Pug. They read cultish books like *Dream Stealer* and many more. They were into computer games. They plotted against real and imagined enemies. They had fun clambering over the assault course, competing against each other, and enjoying the buzz of being together. Above all, however, they were still waiting for Oliver to inspire them, and to reward them.

'We're not ready,' said Pug uneasily.

'I've had this idea,' said Oliver quietly.

'What is it?' Pug looked suspicious.

Oliver gazed up into his rival's large, squashed-looking face – the features that had earned him his nickname – sensing and enjoying his unease. You reckoned you had me sussed, didn't you, he thought. But you haven't, Pug. You really haven't. 'What if we get somebody else in? Someone who'll do exactly what we say. Like Jack Parsons?'

'What makes you think he'll do exactly what you say?'

'He owes me.'

'What does he owe you?'

'Jack broke into the library and nicked some program disks from one of the computers.'

'How do you know that?'

'He tried to sell me a pirated disk.'

'Takes one to know one,' Pug grinned.

'What's that meant to mean?' asked Oliver indignantly.

'What did you say to him?'

'I didn't want any disks.'

'Is he afraid you'll grass him?'

'I *know* he'll do what I say,' Oliver said firmly.

'So what's the plan?'

Was Pug looking at him with a new respect, Oliver wondered. Did he regard him as a criminal mastermind? Or just a loser getting in too deep?

'Jack could tell Ryan about the rink.'

'Great!' said Pug. 'He'll turn up with his own private army.'

'Why don't you shut up, Pug?'

'So what else will Jack tell Ryan?'

'That he wants to suss out the rink with him so they can make a plan to come back with reinforcements and –'

'Have a go.'

'You got it. Jack's got a bike. Ryan's got a bike. They'll cycle over to the Esso petrol station. Then they'll meet Denny.'

'Why him?'

'Denny could say that he's fed up with us – that we're just a load of geeks. So Jack goes home and Denny and Ryan cycle on together to the Bantam. Then we jump Ryan.'

Pug looked even more uneasy, and Oliver was delighted. 'Then what?'

'He'll get a nasty shock, won't he?'

Greg tossed and turned, unable to sleep. Mum had been full of praise for him, but only after she had got Rachel to sleep.

Anger surged, pounding in his chest like a solid object he'd swallowed and couldn't get rid of. If Rachel had never been born, life would be so much better. Even in London.

A fresh start? His parents might look at it that way, but he didn't. Greg only saw a bad start, so bad that he was pushed aside and of no importance any more. His rage increased and he sat up, sweating and clammy, as if he had a fever, finding the walls of the room bulging and then leaning towards him. He *had* to get out of bed, find somewhere cool where he could breathe properly and calm down.

Greg got up and hurried to the door.

Once he was out on the landing, he felt less claustrophobic, and he stood still, breathing deeply, listening to the silence. Then the peace was broken by a tiny murmuring and a muffled cry.

Greg began to walk slowly down the landing to Rachel's nursery.

'We've decided to bring the plan forward,' explained Oliver, with a confidence he didn't feel. Despite the lateness of the hour, the Geeks weren't worried. They often stayed late at the rink, enjoying the feeling of being out when everyone else was in bed. Their parents had given up on telling them off; they all had keys and only went home when they felt like it.

Oliver was standing on the edge of the rink, the Geeks sitting below him, looking younger, more childish than he had seen them before. In fact they just looked like ineffective kids. How could this bunch of idiots ever put his plan into action? 'We're going to get Jack to set Ryan up.' Oliver began to explain and the Geeks listened, giving nothing away. At the end, Oliver turned to Denny and asked, 'OK by you?'

'He could suss me out,' Denny complained, looking wary. 'And what's the hurry anyway?'

Oliver sighed, trying to keep his patience. 'So far you lot aren't getting a penny out of this,' he said. 'You need a reward.'

'How?' demanded Hassan, interested now, as they all were.

Oliver's mind worked furiously. He had to do better than

suggest a bit of shoplifting. He had to convince them he was somebody. A more ambitious somebody than they suspected. 'Thought we might do the corner shop on Derby Road.'

There was a wall of silence. Pug looked shattered and Oliver was pleased.

'I don't get you,' he said.

Of course he didn't, thought Oliver. Pug was simply up to his old trick of public testing, anxious to undermine, to make him look a fool.

But having taken the initiative, Oliver was determined to hang on. 'Mr Williams banks on Fridays. I've been watching him for weeks.'

In fact this was totally untrue, but Oliver was determined to upstage Pug, to upstage them all with what he felt was a convincing lie. What he was going to do when they had successfully dropped Ryan was just another hazy, yet to be solved problem. Ryan was his objective. Everything else, including the Geeks, could go to hell when that was accomplished. A life of crime wasn't his future, but he could easily make promises to these scum-bags.

'So what do we do?' demanded Pug. 'Take the money and run?'

'There's a lot of it,' said Oliver.

'He'll recognise us.'

'Oh yes,' said Oliver sarcastically. 'Of course he will. I was thinking of doing the job in school uniform.'

Pug looked disconcerted as the others laughed.

'What *are* you going to do then?' asked Denny quietly.

'I'm going to provide overalls and stocking masks,' said Oliver hurriedly.

'Where from?' asked Pug.

'I'll find them.'

'And then?'

'We'll grab the money as he leaves the shop and leg it.'

'Equal shares?' asked Denny.

Oliver nodded and felt the interest and confidence in his leadership grow. Pug frowned slightly, and then said, 'How much does Williams take to the bank?'

'I don't know.' Oliver made sure he didn't sound too glib. He had to be convincing. 'But it's a week's takings. Bound to be worth having.'

'When do we do the job?' asked Denny.

'The week after we get Ryan.' Oliver looked around at the Geeks and knew he had them. He felt a surge of glorious power. Quite what he was going to do when they found out he had no intention of mugging Mr Williams at all didn't even enter his head. Look after the present, Mum had often said, and the future will take care of itself.

.

Just after midnight Greg opened the door of the nursery, and in the dim light gazed down at his baby sister who was lying on her back, happily kicking her feet in the air, smiling up at him, making a gurgling sound.

Why are you taking over, Greg found himself thinking. Why did you make us come to London? It's your fault.

Suddenly Greg found tears pricking at the back of his eyes. It's not fair, he thought, gazing steadily down at Rachel, hating her.

Sensing his aggression, the baby screwed up her face and began to howl, the crying high and insistent, swelling in volume until Greg could hardly bear the thin, shrill, plaintive sound.

He heard his parents' bedroom-door opening and the padding of feet across the landing carpet.

As his mother came into the room, Greg wheeled round guiltily.

'What on earth are you doing in here?' she demanded impatiently, the words an accusation.

'I just – I just heard Rachel crying and came to see what I could do.'

'You should have called me.'

'I thought – I wanted you to get some rest.'

His mother seemed to relax a little. 'That was good of you.' Then she seemed to think again. 'But what were you going to do?'

'Dunno,' mumbled Greg miserably.

'She needs feeding,' said his mother, picking up the bawling baby.

'I'm sorry,' said Greg.

'What for?'

'Coming in.'

'Don't be daft.' Her voice softened. 'She *is* your sister. I'm glad you want to help her.'

'But you're right – there's nothing I can do.' Greg's voice was harsh and challenging.

'Unless you can give her a feed, I don't see there *is* much you can do.' His mother tried to make a joke of it all.

'I can't,' said Greg flatly.

'No.' She paused. 'Is there something wrong?'

'Why should there be?'

'You sound a bit –'

'What?'

'Never mind. I should go back to bed and get some beauty sleep. I'll take Rachel into our bed.'

I bet you will, thought Greg, following her out on to the landing. He went back to bed without saying good night and lay awake again, his jealousy raging. His parents seemed to have no time for him these days. They used to run him around in the car to his sports fixtures, for instance. Now they hardly seemed to notice him. All they thought about was Rachel. It wasn't fair.

FOUR

'Oi! You!'

Greg turned to see Sean Dexter striding across the playground towards him.

'I owe you.' Sean still looked pasty-faced and he was walking with a slight limp.

'That's OK.'

'Want to have a laugh?'

Was he offering friendship, wondered Greg. Suddenly, he felt wary for a reason he couldn't understand. 'What sort of laugh?'

'A real laugh.' Sean winked at him. 'A laugh against the Geeks. They grassed us. And they were the ones who gave me and Tim the Drop. They were after Ryan too, but this time *they* got grassed.' Sean chuckled and some of the colour returned to his cheeks. It was a warm day of sticky heat and there was no wind. Sean smelt of sweat.

'Who grassed them?'

'Some little kid. The Geeks wanted him to set Ryan up, kidnap him or something, but he told on them. Now we're going to have a laugh.'

Sean spoke with such hatred that Greg found him unnerving. The head was right. The school had gone bad.

'Where?'

'Down the field. Coming?'

Despite his apprehension, Greg felt tempted. He had always been drawn to risk and excitement. OK, so he'd been happy in Swanage, but there had often been times when he felt contentment was a bit flat. Yet since he had moved to London, Greg had felt increasingly lonely. Sean was offering to include Greg in his gang. He was inviting him to join in. Although Sean seemed a bit aggressive, Greg desperately wanted to make some friends.

'Come on then!' Sean began to run and Greg followed, feeling as if they were heading for some kind of spectacle. Was someone being fed to the lions?

A laughing, whooping, cat-calling group was dragging a thin boy with a pony-tail along the grass by his legs, and although he kept kicking out, his assailants' grip on his ankles was too strong.

Greg could see one or two casual spectators hurrying away as he came up and realised that no one wanted to get involved. So what was he doing here?

Suddenly, as if at an unspoken command, they let go of the boy's legs and one of them began to kick him in the side. Instinctively, the boy rolled himself into a tight ball, grunting with pain as the kicking seemed to get harder.

'Who is he?' demanded Greg, horrified by the apparent viciousness of the attack.

'Oliver Cole,' said Sean delightedly.

Greg realised that this was the Geek leader he had been told about and gazed down at him curiously. He looked a bit of a weirdo.

'Why is he getting a kicking?' Was this the good laugh he had been promised? Greg felt nauseated.

'He tried to set Ryan up.'

'Who's Ryan?'

'The guy with the boots.'

'He's had enough,' said Greg.

The tall boy with the boots and the fair hair looked up. 'Who's this then?'

'Greg.' Sean was cryptic.

Ryan nodded and kicked Oliver Cole again, and so did his companion. 'This is my other mate, Tim.' Amazingly, Ryan was making casual introductions as he continued to mete out his punishment, but the other boys involved seemed to have been made anxious by the interruption and began to walk slowly, almost stealthily, away. 'And this is Cole. Right bastard.' He kicked again and Oliver made a choking sound.

'He's had enough,' Greg repeated.

'He's never had enough.' Ryan's voice was bitter.

'You'll be in trouble,' said Greg. 'You'll hurt him. Bad.'

'Like he did Tim and Sean? Like he was planning to do to me?'

'He's had enough,' Greg insisted. 'You can see he has.'

There was something in his voice that made Ryan pause.

'Maybe you're right,' said Ryan regretfully, looking down at Oliver's hunched figure.

Ryan and Tim continued to gaze down at their gasping victim while Sean hovered, as if he regretted being a mere spectator. Then they all three began to stroll away.

'Thanks for what you did for Sean,' Ryan said over his shoulder. 'You're one of us.'

Greg said nothing, and as they disappeared down the playing field, he crouched down beside Oliver Cole. 'The bell's gone,' he said ineffectively.

Oliver dragged himself to his feet, groaning, wiping at the blood that was now drying on his upper lip.

'You'd better wash your face.'

Oliver looked at him properly for the first time. 'It's a pity you had to interfere. That bastard Sean should have been left hanging.'

'Did you really string him up?' asked Greg curiously, wanting to know more.

'With a little help from my friends.' He was holding his stomach.

'What did Ryan do to you?'

'He flushed an important – he flushed a pendant of mine down the toilet.' Oliver was wincing with pain as he walked back across the grass. 'You'd better get going – or you'll be in trouble.'

'You going to see the nurse?'

'No way.'

'Why not?'

'It'll make me feel worse. I'll clean myself up.' Oliver paused. 'Something went wrong.'

'What was that?' asked Greg curiously.

'Someone let me down.' He paused and then said with surprising warmth, 'I'd like to talk to you, but not now. I don't want to get you into trouble. Don't worry, I'll sort myself out.' Greg glanced at Oliver's bloodied face and the hand now pressed to his side. 'I'm grateful to you for rescuing me.'

'That's OK.'

'You're quite the hero, aren't you? With all your rescuing.'

Greg couldn't work out whether Oliver was being sarcastic or not, and Oliver seemed to pick up on his thoughts. 'But I like heroes. I'd like to be a hero. Why don't we be friends?' Then he turned away and began to run.

Greg watched him go. Oliver *was* a weirdo, and there was something about him that made Greg's skin crawl. At the same time, even more curiously, he wanted to find out more about him. He was a risky person to know, and Greg liked that idea. He needed a friend, too. Even if it *was* Oliver.

Ryan and Oliver weren't in any of Greg's classes – nor were Tim or Sean – which was a good thing, Greg reflected the following day. Greg was still shocked by the brutality of Oliver's beating. There had been fights in Swanage but never like that, and no one had been hung up by the ankles over a filthy lavatory pan. Did this go on all the time in London, or was St Peter's an exception?

'Don't sit there day-dreaming, Greg,' yelled Mr Rattan, the history teacher. 'Every moment of your time is precious here – if you want to pass any exams that is.'

Greg tried to pull himself together but it was difficult. What with rescuing Sean, being neglected by his parents and then watching Oliver getting such a brutal kicking, he felt in a state of sustained shock.

Ryan was much harder than Greg's old mates, but he also seemed the kind of person he could be friendly with and he certainly needed friends. Ryan was aggressive, but at least he was normal – unlike Oliver.

On the other hand, he was still curious about Oliver. Was he really Adam Anlott's son or was he just a fantasy merchant? There was something dangerous about him and Greg was interested in that danger. What could it be? How far did the danger go?

The last thing he wanted was to be permanently on his own. But Greg didn't want to be associated with a running battle that had got badly out of control. And why did Oliver want to talk to him again? What about? Indeed, why did Oliver want to be a friend at all? Ryan and Oliver. Greg's thoughts were confused, and the more he tried to think about it all, the more confused he became.

Ryan and his friends might well have been brutal, but

what about Oliver? How could anyone do what he had done to Sean and Tim? Greg vividly remembered Sean hanging upside down in the old toilets, beating on the seat, his face blackish-red.

Greg shuddered and tried to get on with his work, but his head throbbed as he looked at the worksheet on Oliver Cromwell. To hell with history. Wasn't it all to do with bloodshed anyway? War after war after war. Treason and deceit and people betraying each other, just like the present. No one had learnt anything.

Ryan and Oliver were the products of that history and their battle was in full spate. Then Greg remembered Rachel. Wasn't his baby sister the enemy within?

Greg knew he had closed his mind to the open warfare between his own parents before Rachel's birth. The baby had become their peacemaker, and Greg didn't want to think about that. But he had to admit that life had suddenly become more interesting. Nothing like this had happened to him in Swanage, which was maybe only a paradise because he wasn't there. The realisation made him feel uneasy, as if he had just betrayed himself.

'Hello, Greg.'

Greg jumped as he walked down the corridor towards his locker. 'Hi.'

Oliver smiled. 'I knew where you were.'

'Sorry?'

'I knew you were in history.'

'How?'

'I looked you up on the timetable.'

'How?' repeated Greg, sounding stupid.

'It's in the staff room.'

'But how –'

'The chart's on the wall. The staff room's mostly empty in lesson time, and if anyone *had* asked I'd have made up some reason for being in there. I'm good at that.'

'Are you?' Greg felt trapped. Why had Oliver gone to all that trouble just to waylay him?

'I thought we'd have a talk.'

'Wait a minute. Let's get this straight. You went to all that trouble just to find me?'

'I didn't want to waste any time.'

'I see.' Greg was astounded. It was as if Oliver had become some kind of secret agent.

'Where shall we go? What about behind the lab?'

'OK.' Greg felt as if he was being pushed into something. But what was it? Oliver had gone to a lot of trouble to find him. Shouldn't he be flattered? 'What do you want to talk about?'

'Let's wait till we get there, shall we?'

Greg was very taken aback by Oliver's tone. He sounded just like his mother. She often said stuff like that. 'Wait and see', or 'We'll talk about that later', and when she added 'shall we?' the words always sounded threatening.

FIVE

Greg felt self-conscious as he followed Oliver through the playground, for Oliver made no attempt to walk beside him but imperiously led the way. There was something out of control about him that made Greg cautious. More than cautious – alarmed even. Oliver had such a strange personality that Greg found him menacing. He hoped they wouldn't run into Ryan or Sean or even the largely unknown Tim. They would think he had sided with their enemy.

Oliver walked on confidently, tall and lanky and purposeful under the bright blue sky, pushing his way through the crowd. He showed little sign of any injury from the previous day and Greg suddenly wondered if the kicking had been as serious as he had thought. Had Oliver and Ryan both been playing some kind of game?

Oliver increased his pace and Greg hurried after him, not wanting to be left behind. Immediately he felt a surge of irritation. Why *was* he following Oliver as if he was his servant? The realisation came to him slowly. He was pleased to have been singled out. While Oliver and Ryan both sought his friendship he was able to escape from the ignominy of being a person no one wanted to know. 'You're one of us,' Ryan had said. But Oliver was a one-off.

★

Oliver's face was swollen and cut as he turned to Greg behind the lab, and Greg felt ashamed of suspecting him and Ryan of playing games.

'How are the ribs?'

'They're OK.' Oliver clearly didn't want to waste any time. 'Ryan's an animal,' he said and then paused, waiting for Greg's reaction.

'Is he?'

'You saw what he did.'

'I saw what *you* did.' Greg was determined to assert himself.

Oliver frowned. 'Maybe you don't quite understand,' he said, as if excusing Greg's ignorance.

'What should I understand?'

'It's all a question,' said Oliver slowly, 'of who's in the right.'

There was a long silence during which Greg struggled for a reply. Then he gave up and opted for safer ground. 'Why do they call you the Geeks?' he asked curiously.

'Because we're different. We're not mindless, like the Sweats.'

'What makes you think they're mindless?'

'Has Ryan spoken to you?' Oliver was immediately both hostile and suspicious.

'Only once,' said Greg evasively.

'About me?'

'He doesn't like you.'

'I wouldn't think so.' Oliver smiled for the first time. 'He likes sport.'

'So do I.' Greg suddenly felt afraid. Oliver was staring straight at him and his eyes were wide and innocent, but strangely blank. It was like talking to someone whose mind was set in concrete. There was no perception of other people at all.

'Ryan's got it in for us. Always has had,' said Oliver.

'Who's us?'

'You must meet the others sometime.' Oliver was casual now. Too casual. 'Why don't you join?'

'Join what?'

'My – group?' Oliver seemed to hesitate. 'I won't tell you where we meet. Not yet.'

'What's in it for me?' Greg began to play him along a little. The Geeks sounded a mysterious bunch. Maybe he should try and find out more about them. They sounded risky, like Oliver. He had asked around and no one seemed to know what they got up to. He felt a vague sense of attraction. Here was something that could alleviate his loneliness.

'I just think you'd enjoy some company. You're not a natural loner, are you?'

Greg felt shaken. What had Oliver noticed? Had he been watching him ever since he had arrived at the school? 'What about this kid who caused you all that trouble?'

'Jack? He's nothing. A nobody.'

'He wasn't a member of the Geeks?'

'No chance. He's a mindless moron – like the Sweats.'

'Hanging people upside down isn't a game,' said Greg, and then wished he hadn't sounded so smug.

'Maybe not,' replied Oliver without a trace of emotion. 'But you don't know what they did to us.' He changed the subject smoothly, slipping into a slightly different gear as if he didn't want any questions about 'what they did to us'. 'By the way, do you like keeping fit?'

'Sure.' Greg was mystified now.

'Not mindless sport, I hope.' The word 'mindless' cropped up a lot in Oliver's conversation.

Greg allowed a silence to develop, but Oliver seemed to be quite unfazed, his hands in his pockets, rocking back on his heels a little.

In the end Greg felt forced into taking the initiative. 'I don't get you.'

'We thought we'd toughen ourselves up a bit. Get some muscle.'

'So –'

'We built an assault course. Like the army.'

'That sounds –' Greg searched for the word – 'exciting.' Suddenly he felt trapped again, guessing that Oliver was going to issue an invitation that he might find hard to refuse.

Greg remembered a film he had seen on TV ages ago that had impressed him. *The Godfather*, with Marlon Brando as the Mafia leader. There was something of the Godfather in Oliver.

'Want to try it out?'

'I might.' And indeed he might. The element of risk was there. Did he want to live dangerously for a while?

'Want to meet my dad?' Oliver grinned as he abruptly changed the subject.

Greg felt as if he was being played with, manipulated. 'Er–'

'You know who he is? Ever read the *Dream Stealers*?'

'Yes.'

'Like them?'

'They're bestsellers.' Again Greg side-stepped.

'They certainly are. They're written by my dad. Adam Anlott.'

'He's your dad?'

'Why not? He's got to be someone's dad.'

'Not necessarily.'

'Well, he is mine.' Oliver's eyes were no longer blank. Greg could detect, or thought he could detect, a sudden hostility.

'You serious?'

'Of course I'm serious.'

'Why's he got a different name from you?'

'It's a pseudonym. A made-up name. For his writing.'

'I'd like to meet him.'

'We'll see.' There was a pause. Then Oliver said, 'I'll have to talk to the others.'

'What about?'

'Joining my group.'

'I don't get you,' repeated Greg dully.

'You don't get a lot, do you?' Oliver was impatient now. 'I'm talking about you joining the Geeks.'

'It's a bit of a nerdy name, isn't it?' asked Greg. 'I don't think I want to be a Geek.' He wasn't going to accept just like that. It would be fun playing hard to get.

'You'd enjoy it.' Oliver laughed, but for the first time Greg thought he could detect a hint of uncertainty. 'Actually I invented the name. It sounded rather – weird. Anyway – it's a long way from "The Sweats", isn't it? They've got a really pathetic name.' There was a long pause. 'I could fight you,' said Oliver, coming closer. The challenge was yet another surprise.

'I don't want to fight.'

'Don't you ever fight?'

'Only if I have to.' What kind of game was he playing now? His continuous change of tactics was completely illogical and seemed almost unhinged. Is he off his trolley, wondered Greg – or is he just winding me up? He hoped it was the latter. But there was still something about Oliver that made his skin crawl, that made him feel cold inside.

Oliver stepped even closer. 'If I did fight you, I'd win.'

'Why are you so sure?' asked Greg curiously.

'I've toughened myself up, haven't I?'

'You weren't tough enough yesterday,' Greg pointed out provocatively.

'It was six against one,' Oliver said indignantly. 'You don't have to join if you don't want to. If you're not up to it,' he added mockingly.

Greg didn't reply.

'You're better off a Geek than a Sweat,' said Oliver.

'I'm not a groupie.'

'Then stay a loner.'

'I'm *not* a loner.' Greg was on the verge of losing his temper, but he suddenly pulled back, realising that was what Oliver might want. In the space of a few minutes, he had manipulated him in so many different ways that it was really unsettling – and deeply confusing. 'You don't have to join a group to have friends,' Greg said mildly.

'Who *are* your friends?'

'I haven't got any. Yet.'

'So you live in hope.'

'Why not?' Greg was annoyed to hear how defensive he sounded.

'I'm sure it won't be long. After all, you rescued Sean. You're quite the hero.' Now he was mocking again.

'What would you have done?'

'Passed by on the other side,' laughed Oliver. 'I'd have let him swing.'

'Why do you hate them so much?' Greg deliberately wanted to sound as if he had hardly heard a word Oliver had said.

'Ryan's the serpent.'

'What?'

'Satan's serpent.'

'Are you crazy?'

Oliver suddenly reached out and pushed Greg in the chest. The push was hard and he was surprised at such strength coming from Oliver's gawky frame. 'Yes,' he said. 'I'm a nutter, didn't you know?' He laughed again and then back-tracked. 'Can't you see I'm just winding you up?'

'Are you?'

'You couldn't have taken that seriously. If you did, you're a right prat.'

It was Greg's turn to laugh this time. 'Of course I didn't think you were serious,' he lied.

'But I'm serious when I say I'd like you to try our assault course.'

'I'll think about it.'

'Could be a good laugh.'

'Yes.'

'And then there's my dad. Don't you want to meet the rich and famous?'

The bell went and they both started, as if the sound had broken into the different world they had temporarily been sharing.

'I've got to go,' said Greg.

'Think about what I said.'

Greg began to run, deeply relieved to have been released, but curious. Very curious. What did Oliver want with him? And why did he, Greg, want to find out?

SIX

Greg walked home from school. The Wandsworth streets had a bleached, burnt-out look. The sky was steel grey now and the sun a white blob, giving out a dull scorching heat. There hadn't been any rain for weeks and the Council had imposed a hose-pipe ban.

Here, in the overheated suburbs, the grass in the little park was brown. There were old coke cans and hamburger containers in the basin of the fountain and dog muck on the pavements.

The housing estate just outside the school gates had a row of boarded-up shops, and the stained concrete walkways that connected the prison fortresses of residential blocks had ironically been named after birds – Heron House, Gull Rise, Robin's Walk, Crow's Nest and so on.

Greg couldn't get Oliver out of his mind. Strangely, although Oliver made him wary, even afraid, with his relentless anger and demands, there was something else about him that was compelling. There was danger, a danger he wanted to find out more about. Something right out of the ordinary.

He'd had a real basin-full of his mother's determined ordinariness in Swanage, her obsessive respectability and conviction that the neighbours were always watching and waiting to pronounce on her family's behaviour and appearance. An elderly neighbour, Mrs Harman, was seen by Mum as some kind of arbiter of respectability. She would often lament, 'If Mrs Harman sees you like that, what on earth is she going to think?' This could apply to the clothes Greg was wearing, the way he was playing with his friends outside the house or tinkering with his bike in the front garden. Mrs Harman's potential outrage also applied to his father, and, in particular, to his habit of cheerfully whistling as he walked down to the commuter station nearby, briefcase swinging in time to his step. 'What's Mrs Harman going to think if you make that kind of racket as you pass her door?'

Eventually Mum had forced Dad to whistle under his breath, which was a much more irritating habit.

But Dad was just as bad in his own way, thought Greg. He had always wanted Greg to join clubs – and to exactly obey their rules. Like in the sailing club, he could never go inside without a tie, in the squash club he always had to wear white, and in the rugby club he had to address older members as 'sir'.

To Greg all this seemed ridiculous, but to his father it was of paramount importance. Greg wasn't a natural rebel and he enjoyed the sports his father encouraged him to play. What he didn't enjoy was their silly, pathetic rules.

As Greg walked along, he remembered how his parents had got on each other's nerves in small ways, for although they were unified in wanting to conform, they had opposing views about how to do so – and this had continuously led to trouble between them, usually taking the form of small bickering arguments that developed into bigger arguments and later into bitter quarrels. The rows had made Greg sick with misery, but although the move and the birth of Rachel seemed to have patched things up, for him they had been replaced by a different kind of pain.

On reflection, Greg thought, the past had been far less of a paradise than he would have liked to remember.

'Day-dreaming?' asked Ryan as he cycled up beside him.

Greg jumped, realising he had been crawling along at a snail's pace.

'Suppose so.'

'I saw you with Oliver.'

'Yeah?' Greg felt a wave of exhaustion, realising he was about to hear the 'other side's' point of view. Well, he couldn't say he was unpopular now. Here were two people anxious to claim him as their own and they both had hangers-on, none of whom he had really met except for Sean who had been hanging upside down at the time. The play on words amused him and he grinned.

Ryan frowned as if he suspected Greg of sending him up, and he quickly wiped the smile off his face.

'He button-holed me.'

'At the back of the lab?'

'Were you down there too?'

'I saw you following him. Oliver likes to lead.' Ryan paused. 'You'd better be careful. He's a bit of a nutter.'

'In what way?'

'He thinks his father's Adam Anlott.'

'Maybe he is.'

Ryan laughed confidently. 'He couldn't be.'

Greg didn't want to say any more.

'But it's not just that,' Ryan continued. 'I'm fed up with him sending me his stupid notes.' He looked uneasy.

'What notes?' Greg was instantly much more alert.

'They're sick. Do you want to see the latest?'

'Why not?'

Leaning on his bike outside the shopping arcade, Ryan got out his wallet and pulled out a crumpled piece of toilet paper.

The words had been cut from a newspaper and carefully, methodically, stuck down with glue. The message read: *WE'LL BE STRETCHING YOUR NECK.*

'I've had a lot of those,' said Ryan casually.

'Anyone else – yet – been pestered like this?'

'Only me.' He smiled but deliberately avoided eye contact. 'They're nothing to get steamed up about.'

'Oliver doesn't like you much, does he?'

'I wouldn't expect him to. He's just a nerd.' Greg wasn't so sure. Oliver was far more than a nerd. He was a mystery. A creepy mystery. You couldn't just brush him aside like that.

'Do the notes come in the post?' he asked.

'No. They're usually shoved on my desk, or occasionally stuck on my bike. This one was wrapped round the brake.'

'There's no actual proof Oliver wrote them.'

'I don't need proof.' Ryan gave a confident grin that seemed false. 'He needs zapping again.'

'He's got himself into a state.' Greg offered a get-out, but Ryan wasn't having any.

'He's a nutter.'

'What started all this?'

'Hasn't he told you?' Ryan asked mockingly.

'He said you'd picked on him.'

'We had a few laughs, that's all.' Ryan paused. 'Oliver hates Sweats. Especially me and Tim and Sean.'

'What's a Sweat?' asked Greg innocently.

'Anyone who plays sport and wants to join the crowd.'

That makes Dad a Sweat, thought Greg. 'Is that why you got suspended? Having a go at Oliver?'

'We did something stupid.' Ryan looked embarrassed.

'What?'

'We bullied some young kids.'

'Why?'

'We needed some more sponsorship for a charity football fixture. They were well-off kids.' Ryan shrugged. 'It was a stupid idea, and I'm sorry about it. I got into really big trouble at home.' He paused. 'Oliver grassed us.'

'So you hate him.'

'You bet I do.'

'I reckon the feeling's mutual,' said Greg. He glanced at Ryan again and only received another mocking grin. He didn't know what to think. Should Ryan really be taking Oliver seriously? Or deep down was he afraid? It was impossible to tell.

'What was he talking to you about?' Ryan sounded too casual this time.

'His dad.'

'And?'

'How he'd built some muscle on this assault course they've got together. Oliver asked me to join, but I said I didn't want to be a Geek.'

Ryan was stony-faced. 'Do you mean that?'

'I didn't fancy it.'

They both laughed.

'Are you scared of him?' asked Greg suddenly.

'No way.'

'I am,' he admitted. 'He wanted me to fight him.'

'Did you?'

'Why should I?'

'So you think he's a nutter too?' Ryan looked hopeful.

'I couldn't make him out. But I *was* slightly scared of him because he's so weird. What are his mates like?'

'Misfits – like him. Weird bunch.'

But that, to Greg, made them sound interesting. 'They're all in training then – on this assault course they've built?'

Greg was seeking more information and at the same time trying to gauge just how Ryan really felt.

'I've no idea.' He laughed contemptuously. 'I don't like getting these notes though,' he admitted suddenly.

'Go to the head.'

'I can't.'

'Why not? Oliver grassed you.'

Ryan didn't reply, and Greg wondered again if Ryan and Oliver were going through some strange ritual. Were they having fun?

'Then what *are* you going to do?'

Ryan didn't reply directly. Then he said, 'Do you want to play football?'

Greg stared at him. It was like Oliver asking him to join the Geeks but in a much more acceptable way.

'There's this Saturday morning league starting. Interested?'

Greg nodded.

'We're going to play in the park across the road in the autumn, but right now we're doing some practice on the school field.'

'Who's in charge?'

'Bob Burnett. He's head of PE at school. Plays in a league himself. Met him yet?'

'Yes – he's a great guy.' Greg had liked him immediately.

'You on then?'

'What time?'

'Ten-thirty, Saturday.'

'OK.'

They began to move on, Ryan wheeling his bike alongside Greg, clearly not anxious to let him go.

Eventually Greg broke the silence. 'So what about these Geeks? What have they been up to then?' he asked provocatively, needing to see how Ryan *really* evaluated them.

'Not a lot. Only strung up Sean and Tim.' Ryan paused. 'They act like kids in some secret society. They've got passwords and coded messages and they spy on us.' He tried to sound mocking but somehow failed.

'Spy?'

'Like watch round corners. They can really get to you.' Ryan paused and became more reflective. 'You can feel their – their dislike. Particularly Oliver's.'

'Why *do* they hate Sweats so much?'

'Because they want to be like us. Why do you think they're trying to toughen themselves up?' Ryan was contemptuous again.

'Where is this assault course then?'

'I'm not sure, but I guess I was soon going to find out.'

'How?'

'Jack Parsons. Oliver tried to recruit him.'

'Is he a Sweat?'

'No. Maybe a Sweat in the making. Except Oliver thought he might have been a Geek in the making. Bit of a mix-up all round.' Ryan grinned again. 'Jack's only a kid in Year Seven.'

'So what happened?'

'Jack's keen on football. I gave him a few tips once. He came along the other day and said that Oliver was going to pay him to set me up.'

'How?' asked Greg curiously. The whole business was like a maze of deception. The trouble was that it was also like a fascinating game. But because he'd seen how disturbed Oliver was, Greg knew it ran deeper, much deeper than that.

'Something about the Esso station. Then someone was going to take over – and I don't know what was going to happen after that. Neither did Jack. But I reckon I was going to get done over one way or the other.' Ryan laughed.

'So you and your mates gave Oliver a good kicking.'

'We held back a bit. Got to be careful.'

'I wondered about that.' Got to be careful about what, wondered Greg. The head teacher? Oliver himself?

'Then you came along,' said Ryan softly. 'And did your hero bit again. Do you feel you *have* to go round rescuing people all the time?'

'I was on the spot. That's all.'

There was a brief silence.

'So *are* you going to see Oliver again?'

'I don't know.' Greg wasn't going to be told what to do by either of them.

'You'll turn up for training?'

'I'll think about it.'

Ryan seemed relieved. It's as if they're competing for me, thought Greg. It was also the complete reverse of being lonely. Or was it? He suddenly realised that he felt just as isolated as before.

SEVEN

'You're not going to sit reading that trash, are you?'

Greg looked up from *Dream Stealer 5* to see his father standing over him.

Rachel was crying upstairs. Mum was with her. Naturally.

'I like it,' he said defensively.

'For God's sake –' His father seemed to be in an irritable mood for the first time since they had moved. What had gone wrong?

'What's the matter with it?'

'Tell me the plot.'

'It's about this boy who has these weird dreams about being in hell and the Dream Stealer pinches one of his dreams and gives it to this crook who won't confess to a murder. So the crook dreams the hell dream every night and it gets to him so much that he gives himself up – but the boy who originally dreamt the hell dream turns out to be his cousin and he finds out –'

'Stop!' Dad covered his ears. 'I've never heard so much rubbish.'

'I enjoy it.'

'Hardly literature, is it?'

'I don't know.' Greg was getting irritable now. Why

couldn't Dad get off his back?

'If only you read more intelligent stuff, then maybe your half-term report would have been more up to scratch. I mean, I appreciate you had the guts to rescue that kid, but work's work and you'll never pass any exams if –'

'What does the report say?'

Silently his father handed the folded piece of paper across. Greg had forgotten St Peter's gave half-term reports. At his last school they had been given their reports to take home, but St Peter's had obviously decided to go to the expense of sending the reports in the post. Did the head reckon the pupils were deliberately going to lose them? What a rotten trick, he thought as he read on, only to discover that he seemed to have done badly in all subjects, and at the bottom of the page his head of year had written:

Gregory is a highly intelligent boy with great potential. I realise that he has had to face considerable changes, moving from Dorset to London, and entering the school two years late which has been hard on him both socially and academically. Nevertheless, Gregory seems to dream his way through class when he should be trying to make up lost ground. He must take his work more seriously in the next half of the term. I look forward to Gregory reaching his full potential.

'It's not all bad,' said Greg.

'It's not all good,' replied Dad.

'What do you expect?'

'Sorry?'

'I said, what do you expect?' Exhausted by his encounters at school, furious that his reading habits had been criticised and now upset by the report, Greg suddenly lost his temper.

'I don't understand.' Dad's voice was cold.

'You uproot me – and then expect the earth –'

'We uprooted ourselves. It was a mutual decision.'

'Rubbish!' yelled Greg. 'Utter bloody rubbish. I was happy at home. I hate it here.'

'Keep your voice down. Rachel will –'

'I don't care how hard she cries. In fact I don't care if she busts a gut.'

'Greg –' His father was more alarmed than angry now.

'All you do is make a fuss about her.'

'We never –'

'And you don't give a damn for me!' Greg shouted, and Rachel began to wail upstairs.

'Greg – of course we care for you. My new job gives us a lot more financial flexibility. Why don't you join the squash club? It's great fun and there's a junior ladder –'

'The junior ladder sounds a load of crap,' yelled Greg.

'Now look here –' Dad was getting pompous, as he always did when he was angry, and his slightly balding head glowed with perspiration.

'No. You look here. I'm going out.'

Greg could hear Mum coming downstairs, carrying a howling Rachel.

'You haven't finished your homework, so you're not going anywhere – and don't swear at me.'

Greg stood up just as Mum opened the sitting-room door.

'What's going on?' she asked above the sound of Rachel's crying.

'Not a lot,' replied Greg. 'I'm on my way out.'

'Where to?'

'I don't know. A long way from here.' He pointed a shaking finger at Rachel. 'And that brat.'

'*What?*' Mum was completely amazed, not knowing what was going on, or having the slightest chance to understand why hostilities had broken out.

'He's had a lousy report and he can't take it,' snapped Dad.

'But I thought you were doing so well, darling.' She seemed dazed, while Rachel, bright red in the face, tried to out-scream them all.

'I'm not now!' yelled Greg. 'I can't read what I like. I can't do what I like –'

'You certainly can't,' interrupted Dad furiously. 'You're going to do some damn hard work –'

'So are you,' shouted Greg. 'You're going to do a lot more damn hard work finding me.' He pushed past Mum and Rachel.

'Come back here,' yelled Dad.

But Greg ran for the front door, slamming his way out.

★

Greg trudged through the muggy streets, heading for the dusty little park where he intended to hang around until his parents – particularly his father – were out of their minds with worry. But Greg knew his mother would worry much more, particularly as he had said such terrible things about Rachel.

Greg had surprised himself. Had he really bottled up so much anger about his baby sister? *I don't care if she busts a gut.* His own voice rang in his mind, vicious and biting. He glanced down at his watch. It was six pm. How much worrying time should he give his parents? He might have to be out here for hours before he was able to return without losing face.

Greg wished he'd brought *Dream Stealer 5* with him. He was well into it and would have enjoyed flinging himself down on the grass and reading the book to the end. Worse still, he hadn't changed, and wearing his school uniform in the evening in a public place made Greg feel acutely embarrassed. Everyone would take him for a right prat.

Digging his hands into his pockets, scowling and trying to look cool but actually feeling slightly ridiculous, Greg strolled into the park whistling, and then realised he sounded horribly like his father. He'd definitely have to stay out until at least nine pm to make an impact, to show them he meant business and wasn't just some immature little boy with a temper tantrum. But what was he going to do until then?

Greg walked across the parched grass to a grubby-looking bandstand with peeling paint, a survivor from another era. He sat down on the stained, rotting wood and wished he had a cigarette to light – although he hated the smell and had always resisted the habit. Would Mum and Dad be scouring the streets? He didn't think so. Rachel would probably need another feed after her screaming session, and Dad would start watching the football on TV. He didn't give a damn about Greg anyway.

Stretching out flat on his back, Greg closed his eyes against a growing feeling of self-consciousness.

'Excuse me.'

'Mm?'

'Excuse *me* –'

Reluctantly Greg opened his eyes to see an elderly woman with a thickly powdered face standing over him, dressed in a floral frock.

'Yes?'

'Are you well?'

'Well?' Greg was bewildered. 'I'm fine. How are you?' he finished cheekily.

Her lips clamped together in disapproval, forming a thin red line. 'I thought you might be – in need of help.'

Greg sighed. Now he understood. She probably thought he was on drugs and had passed out on the floor of the bandstand. 'I'm OK.'

'You're sure?'

'Just having a bit of a rest. Had a hard day at school.'

She gave him a chilly smile and hurried on, not looking back.

That's her good deed done for the day, thought Greg bitterly as he got to his feet. The old bandstand was obviously too public a place to try and pass the time, so he wandered into a shrubbery which contained a pond full of goldfish. Unlike the rest of the park, the pond was well cared for and there were enormous water lilies in the translucent green water. There was no one else around and Greg sat down on a bench, watching the fish glide lazily through the plants and weed.

Their slow movements succeeded in making him sleepy. His head fell forward on to his chest and Greg relaxed at last.

'Mind if I sit here?'

'Eh?' Greg looked up, his head aching. A man was sitting beside him, middle-aged and wearing a T-shirt and jeans.

'Fine by me,' said Greg warily, conscious that his companion was dressed too young and had pallid white arms and a large belly.

'Nice evening. Bit muggy.'

'Yeah.' Greg wanted to leave, but didn't know how to go about it without appearing rude.

'Just got out of school?'

'Yeah.'

'Where do you go?'

'St Peter's.'

'Play sport?'

'Football.'

There was a silence which became increasingly tense. Then the man slowly got up and began to walk away, whistling. 'See you around,' he said.

Greg watched him until he was out of sight, rigid with anxiety. His parents had warned him, his old school had warned him. Never talk to strangers. Never accept a lift. Never be vulnerable – and he had been, sitting on his own by the pond, just waiting to be preyed upon. Or had he? Maybe the man was as lonely as he was and had just stopped by for a chat. Dimly, he heard a baby crying and then the sound was abruptly cut off so Greg couldn't work out whether he had heard it or not, like he couldn't work out whether the man had been hostile or not. And here he was, still sitting alone, a target for everyone and everything.

Greg shivered as the sun began to set and dark shadows crept around the pond. Something scurried and rustled in the undergrowth and a breeze rippled the surface of the water. He felt clammy with fear, yet he still couldn't bring himself to get up, to leave the isolation behind him, to go back into the park where there were people and safety. He tried to move, willing himself to stand up, but he felt frozen inside and inert outside, like a rock on a beach that had no life of its own but things grew on.

He remembered what it was like to touch soft and furry moss, and shuddered, and then gasped and almost screamed aloud as the wind sent an ice-cream wrapper winding itself around his ankle. It was like a soft, human touch and the scream seemed to be trapped inside him, unable to come out, making him at least overcome his rigidity and struggle shakily to his feet, stumbling, almost falling towards the pond and then running stiff-legged out of the shadows towards the park, still screaming inside.

Greg was still shaking as he walked towards the gates. There was only one place he wanted to go and that was home. It didn't matter about face-saving now. But *did* the man know where he lived? Had he been watching him? Following? Or was he worrying unnecessarily? Applying logic, Greg was sure that it had been nothing at all. Then his fearful confusion grew. If there was nothing to fear, why had the man approached him? Why had he spoken to him? British people didn't speak to strangers, did they? Unless the person had wanted something. Or were just lonely? The buzzing thoughts were like hornets in his head and he still couldn't stop shaking.

Greg began to run towards the gates of the park, welcoming the stench of traffic fumes and the drone of engines. But as he reached the gates, he could see that Oliver was standing there, waiting for him.

★

For a moment Greg seriously considered the possibility of Oliver and the man being in league, each looking out for the other.

Then he dismissed the idea as even more ridiculous than the threat.

'Fancy seeing you.'

'I was waiting for you,' Oliver said ominously.

'How did you know where I was?' Greg dithered, trapped again.

'I phoned home.'

'Whose home?' Greg was confused and afraid, suddenly feeling as if he was being controlled by unknown forces.

'Your home of course. I wanted a word.'

'What do you mean?'

'Don't you understand English? You look as if you've had a shock. What happened?'

'What did you phone my home for?'

'I don't believe it. You *don't* understand English. I phoned because I wanted to talk to you.'

'How did you get the number? We're not in the book yet.'

'I checked it out at school.' For the first time, Oliver was slightly thrown.

'The staff room?'

'The office. The receptionist went out for a minute and –'

'You crept in.'

'Something like that.'

The trap closed again. Oliver had him under surveillance. 'What did you want the number for?'

'Thought it might come in useful.'

'I told you – I don't want to become a Geek.' Greg paused. 'I still don't know how you found me.'

'Your Dad said you'd gone out. Probably down to the park. So I came to look.'

So Dad had guessed where he'd gone. Greg realised this wasn't difficult, for the scruffy little park was the only open space around. So if Dad knew where he was, why hadn't he come to find him? Greg had been right. Dad didn't give a damn for him. He suddenly felt the tears pricking at the back of his eyes and hurriedly blinked them away. He caught Oliver's smile and wondered if he'd noticed.

'What do you want then?'

'I'd like you to meet my mates.'

'I don't want to be a Geek.' Greg suddenly had the humiliating feeling that he must sound like a seven-year-old.

Again Oliver grinned and Greg was sure that he was relishing his anguish.

'You don't have to be. I just thought you might like a go on the assault course.'

'Why should I want to do that?'

'It's cool. For a Sweat –'

'I'm not a Sweat,' snapped Greg.

'Or a Geek.'

'I don't want to be –'

'Or anyone else who likes to take a bit of a risk. Or don't you like taking risks?'

'Where is it then?' Greg wanted out. He'd agree to anything if only he could get home. He was desperate to get away from Oliver.

'We don't want anyone to know where it is.'

'That makes it a bit of a problem for me getting there, doesn't it?'

'We take our secrecy seriously,' said Oliver. 'Very seriously indeed. If I tell you then I don't want you blabbing to anyone else.'

'OK.'

'Especially Ryan.'

'No.' Greg paused. 'Can I ask you a question?'

'What is it?'

'Why are you making such a fuss of me?'

'I don't get you.' But Oliver looked wary.

'Why are you paying me so much attention?'

'You think I fancy you or something?' said Oliver, mockingly.

'I don't know what I think.' Greg was deliberately evasive.

'All right, I'll tell you. It's like I think you could – see what we're about. You'd fit in well.'

'Why?'

'We're all individuals. We don't run with a crowd – like the Sweats.' Greg was about to interrupt, but Oliver hurried on. 'OK, you could be thick enough to be a Sweat. But I hope you won't. You've got too much going for you.'

'I don't want to be a Geek.' Greg knew he needed to be assertive.

'Give us a try.'

'Where's your hide-out then?'

'It's up the other end of the High Road – just behind a closed-down pub called The Bantam.'

'You still haven't told me what this place is.'

'It's an old roller-skating rink. The whole site's waiting to be redeveloped. In the meantime, we've moved in.'

'You're trespassing?'

'No one's noticed. No one ever comes near.'

'I'll see.'

'I'm taking a risk myself,' said Oliver.

'What's that?' Greg wished he could sometimes, just sometimes, predict what Oliver was going to say next. But that seemed impossible.

'I'm confiding in you. I don't want Ryan to know where we hang out.'

'So you said.'

There was a long silence.

Then Oliver asked quietly, 'What happened?'

'When?'

'In the park.'

'Nothing.' Greg began to panic. What *did* he know?

'Something did.' Oliver took his arm and suddenly it seemed like he was years older. Greg shivered. 'You can tell me,' Oliver insisted gently, as if Greg had spoken aloud.

Greg had never felt so lonely, so desperate to have someone on his side. 'Nothing happened,' he snapped.

'Where were you?'

'By the pond.'

'That's a dodgy area.'

'How was I to know? I wanted to think. I'd had a row at home.'

'I'm sorry.' Oliver dropped Greg's arm and said firmly, 'Look – you don't have to be anything but yourself. I'd just like you to drop in and –'

'Did you say "drop"?' asked Greg warily.

'Slip of the tongue.' Oliver looked amused. 'Why don't you just come – see if you like it?'

'OK.'

'When?'

'How about Saturday? In the afternoon. About two.' Oliver paused and then repeated obsessively, 'I'd rather you didn't mention to Ryan that you're coming to see us.'

'I won't tell him.'

'And watch out in the park,' continued Oliver.

'I wouldn't be seen dead in this park again.'

Oliver gave a wolfish grin. 'See you at school tomorrow.'

'See you,' replied Greg. It was as if he had been given permission to leave.

EIGHT

Greg was sure he was going to suffer the ultimate humiliation at home. Not only had he slammed his way out and forgotten his keys, not only had his father known where he would go, not only was he coming home too early – but he had never needed his parents so much and they were bound to let him down. The combined shock of the park and Oliver's ambush had undermined Greg completely. He needed reassurance and a proper talk but, of course, all that was a thing of the past. Rachel got all the attention now.

Grimly, he knocked on the front door, and after what seemed like an interminable delay his father answered, looking tired and slightly impatient.

'So you're back.'

'Yes.'

'Your mother's gone to bed. She's very upset, lying awake, waiting for you to come home.' Dad was getting angry now.

'Is Rachel asleep?'

'Your mother wouldn't be in bed if she wasn't.' Dad pronounced the phrase 'your mother' as if she was some kind of fragile saint.

Greg followed him into the sitting room where the TV

set was gently muttering, and a can of beer was on the table by the sofa. It didn't look as if Dad had exactly got himself into a wild panic while he was out.

Greg sighed. What a fool he'd been to come back so early. If he'd had any guts at all he ought to have stuck it out despite what had happened.

There was a long silence as his father sat down on the sofa again, sipped at his beer and gloomily watched a game show, although the sound was so low he could hardly be able to hear it.

'I didn't mean to upset Mum.'

'Well – you did.'

'I don't like it here – that's all.'

'It's a big "that's all".'

'It's all very well for you,' Greg said vaguely.

'Haven't you got any homework to do?'

Greg didn't trust himself to reply. It wasn't that he was going to lose his temper; all he wanted to do was cry – and go on crying. But he couldn't do that. Not now.

'I'm sorry to hear you're jealous of a helpless baby,' said Dad at last.

'She gets a lot of attention.'

'She has to.'

'I'm going up to my room.'

'To do your homework?'

'To do what I damn well like,' snapped Greg with a brief return to temper.

'Don't speak to me like that.' Dad sounded perfunctory. He seemed too exhausted for another row. 'By the way – a friend of yours phoned. Seemed a nice lad. Quite anxious about you.'

'Who was it?'

'Oliver Cole. Said he was worried that you hadn't made that many friends at school.'

'That's none of his business – and why was he telling you?' Greg felt uneasy and angry at the same time, conscious that tight coils of tentacles were closing in on him.

'He just seemed a potentially good friend, that's all. Said he'd had a lot of trouble with bullying and how much he admired you for rescuing that boy instead of keeping your head down. We *all* admire you for that.'

Greg was silent.

'You've made such a good start. Why are you throwing it all away?'

'I'm not.'

'Anyway, Oliver wants you to meet his mates over the weekend.' Dad used the words 'mates' with a horrible, gut-squirming self-consciousness, and Greg winced, feeling acutely embarrassed.

'I might go.'

'It's no good saying you're the odd man out if you don't make the effort. Your Mum and I –'

'All right,' said Greg, not able to stand any more. 'I'll go and do my homework.'

★

Exhausted and deeply depressed, Greg sat and stared at his homework and then went to bed without saying good night to his father, falling into a deep sleep, only to dream of a monster Rachel who was standing beside his bed blowing herself up until she became a balloon with a tiny head, arms and legs.

Searching for a dream pin – and finding one in his bed – Greg stuck it into Rachel, watching the baby balloon deflate with a horrible squeaking sound.

Then the squeaking was replaced by a faint sighing.

Greg opened his eyes and saw his mother standing at the foot of his bed in her dressing gown.

'Mum?' he half-whispered.

'I couldn't go to sleep until I'd spoken to you.'

Greg sat up. 'I'm sorry,' he said.

She shook her head. 'It's my fault. I can see how left out you've felt.' His mother sat down on the edge of the bed.

'It's OK. I made a fuss.'

'Are you really so lonely? I thought you'd made some friends.'

'I have.'

'You're sure?'

'Yes.' He thought of Ryan and Oliver. Some friends! Suddenly there came Rachel's wailing cry.

'Oh dear,' said his mother, 'I'll have to go. Do you mind?'

'Of course I don't.'

'You're not really –'

'I just got into a temper.'

Rachel's crying intensified and his mother got off the bed. 'I know it hasn't been easy – this move.'

But now he wanted her to go. 'I'm tired, Mum. That's all it is – I've been getting too tired.'

She bent over and kissed him. 'I love you so much, Greg.'

'I love you,' he grunted, closing his eyes. His mum hurriedly left the room as Rachel began to bawl.

'Hello, Greg.'

Oliver was waiting at the front entrance to the school. He looked eager.

'Hi.' Greg sounded grudging.

'I wanted to know how you were.'

'I'm OK.'

'Lucky I was on hand last night.'

'Yeah.'

Just then, Ryan came up with a slightly mocking grin as if he was making his own kind of rescue. Oliver frowned.

'Hi. Greg. OK for the practice on Saturday?'

'Sure. I'm looking forward to it.'

'What about Saturday afternoon?' asked Oliver, the tension in his voice all too obvious.

'I'm fine for that too.'

Oliver began to walk away, his shoulders hunched. He didn't look back.

'You going around with him, then?' asked Ryan, the grin gone.

'He asked me to go over this assault course.'

'What for?'

'I'm not sure. He's going to meet me on his bike and take me there.' Greg wondered why he had just lied to Ryan. Why hadn't he told him about the old roller-skating rink? He was sure to know where it was. Oliver had insisted that he should keep the Geeks' headquarters secret. But why was he obeying him?

As if by instinct, Greg and Ryan both looked round to see Oliver lurking by the bike sheds, watching them, but when he saw they'd seen him, he turned away and walked into school.

'That weirdo – why do you want to go around with him?'

'I don't.'

'Then why did you agree to go over his lousy assault course?'

'I was curious.'

'Be careful.'

'Careful of what?' Greg wondered if Ryan was really concerned or whether he was just stirring.

'Suppose he gives you the Drop?'

'Why should he do that?'

'Because you're in with Sweats like me. In fact –' Ryan suddenly grinned – 'you *are* a Sweat if you're coming to football training.'

Greg considered the situation carefully. Could Ryan be right? A chill swept through him. Then he said, 'I've got a theory about Oliver.'

'What's that then?'

'I think he's spying on me.'

Ryan laughed and then stopped abruptly, his eyes on Greg's. 'What do you mean?'

'He keeps turning up. Now he and his mates have built this assault course. They want to toughen themselves up, don't they?'

'I wonder why.' Ryan seemed to be giving the problem serious thought now.

'So do I.'

Ryan shook his head and shrugged. 'I reckon he's going for the final battle.'

Now it was Greg's turn to ask, 'What do you mean?'

'It's overdue, isn't it? Sweats versus Geeks.'

'Where does that leave me?' wondered Greg involuntarily.

'I'd take one side or the other. Not sit in the middle.'

'I don't want to be on *anyone's* side.'

'Suppose Oliver thinks you are?'

Greg was silent.

'Suppose he thinks you're on our side. Maybe he *is* going to give you the drop.'

'Isn't yours overdue?' Greg tried to laugh, but failed.

'He's saving me till last.'

There was a long pause.

'Suppose he thinks you're on *his* side?' asked Ryan uncertainly.

But Greg didn't want to continue the discussion.

'I want to talk to you.' Oliver's face was dark with sullen anger and Greg immediately felt apprehensive. The day was overcast but hot and humid and the sun was a white speck again, thinly covered with clouds, looking like a small insect.

Oliver had ambushed Greg yet again, this time on his way to the canteen. The smell of chips was overpowering in the heat and so was the sharp aroma of vinegar.

'What is it?'

Oliver seemed to be immensely tall, towering over him broodingly. 'What are you up to?' he said menacingly.

'I don't get you.'

'You and Ryan sending us up?'

'Why should we?'

'I've got friends too, you know,' Oliver said truculently.

'I never see them,' replied Greg dismissively. 'Where do they hang around?' He wanted to get in first. However uneasy Greg felt, he was determined not to be put in the wrong by Oliver.

'That's because I told them to give me a wide berth at school. Geeks are individuals, not a gang.

'So is Ryan,' said Greg. 'None of us likes gangs.'

'So you're going to football training?'

'Why not? I like football.'

'After all I've done for you?' For the first time, Oliver seemed disconcerted.

'What do you mean?'

Oliver hurriedly changed tack. 'I'm just surprised that you're consorting with someone like him.' He now sounded incredibly pompous.

'I know you've had your differences –' Greg tried to be a little more accommodating.

'That's an understatement. He's a thug. Like his friends. Like all Sweats.'

'Why do you have to label people all the time?'

'It helps if you know they're dangerous animals.'

'Come on –'

'They ought to have a sign round their necks that reads *BEWARE – ANIMAL*.' Oliver was smiling maliciously.

'I can play football if I like – I don't need your permission.'

'Are you still on for the afternoon?'

'I don't know –'

'Please.' It was amazing how Oliver suddenly changed from outrage to pleading.

'Suppose you give me the Drop?' Greg half-laughed, trying to take the sting out of what he had just said.

'Who put that idea into your head?'

'Nobody.'

'It was Ryan, wasn't it? Trying to warn you off.'

'What if he did?'

'Look —' Oliver grabbed his shoulder, and once again Greg was surprised and alarmed by the strength of his grip. 'I'm your friend. I wouldn't hurt you. Are you coming or not?'

Greg hesitated. 'OK.'

'Sure?'

'I'm sure.'

'See you at two then. You've remembered the directions I gave you?'

'I've remembered,' said Greg quietly.

'I'm here to protect you.' Oliver was suddenly full of brooding authority. 'Like from the park. Like from Ryan.'

'I don't need protecting,' Greg yelled at him.

'Don't you?' Oliver looked round and Greg suddenly realised everyone was staring at them.

NINE

That night, Mum, clearly making a special effort, cooked Greg a home-made curry (his favourite food), produced cans of coke (his favourite drink) and a video that he hadn't seen.

Greg felt almost guilty and certainly uncomfortable because he knew his parents' eyes were on him, wanting to make sure he knew he was needed, that he was as important as everyone else in the family, just as important as Rachel.

When Rachel began to bellow, Mum rushed upstairs and returned as fast as she could, looking almost guilty, while Dad made stilted conversation, carefully avoiding dangerous subjects like reports and homework.

Eventually, his parents made Greg so tense that he was pleased to go to bed, where he slept soundly and without dreaming.

'Well done, son. That was a nice tackle.'

The coach had been encouraging from the start, but Greg knew that his praise had been hard won. Bob Burnett was young and enthusiastic and expected his players to be thoroughly committed. He stood no nonsense.

'I'm only taking on boys with bottle,' he had told them before they started to train.

'So why are you stupid enough to go down there on your

own?' asked Ryan after the session, returning to the disputed subject with relish. For the first time, Sean and Tim were hanging around too and Greg had got to like both of them, despite their aggression. Tim was quieter and rather unassuming, with red hair and a terrific skill at football. Sean was the opposite, an extrovert who thrived on confrontation. He seemed to have recovered from his grisly experience in the abandoned toilets and hadn't thanked Greg again, as if he wanted to put the experience behind him.

'I want to go alone,' said Greg. It was good to be in the company of Ryan's friends. They were hard, tough, uncomplicated. Or were they? he wondered as he risked another glance without making eye contact. It was something they all avoided, while Oliver's eyes seemed to bore into his all the time.

'Why don't we come with you?' suggested Tim. 'We can all suss them out then.'

'What's the point?' replied Greg. 'Maybe they're not all that bad,' he added. Once again he was determined not to be taken over. He didn't want to be part of any group – however good he felt after the training. He wanted friends, but he didn't want to take sides like Oliver and Ryan so often urged him to do. He was also increasingly worried that Oliver might spread rumours about what might, or might not, have happened in the park. But how could he? Oliver knew nothing and, anyway, nothing had happened.

Yet there was something horribly all-seeing about him. It was as if Oliver had somehow got into his mind. But maybe that was one of the reasons why Greg was so curious about him.

'Not all that bad?' Sean was suddenly bitter, the memory of his ordeal surfacing again. 'They're perverts. They got a real kick out of stringing me up. So you want to be a pervert too, do you?' The friendly atmosphere disappeared so abruptly that it was as if it had never existed.

Greg felt a wave of despair and then anger. 'What did you say?' He moved forward threateningly.

Ryan hurriedly stepped between them. 'Knock it off, you two.'

Sean was breathing in short sharp gasps and Tim grabbed his arm. 'Leave it.' He sounded even more authoritative than Ryan. 'Greg's not your clone.'

Sean unclenched his fists – and then clenched them again. 'Anyone who associates with those creeps needs a good kicking.'

'Shut up –' began Greg, moving towards him again, but Ryan pushed him away.

'Just listen, Sean,' said Tim. 'I got dropped – just like you did. But maybe Greg's right. He might as well go and see for himself. He's got to make up his own mind, hasn't he?'

Greg cycled down the busy arterial road with trucks thundering past him, feeling distinctly alarmed, remembering how worked up Oliver had got after he had seen him talking to Ryan.

Oliver was such a weird mixture – partly soft-soaping, partly trying to bully him. Ryan was the real object of Oliver's hatred and Greg knew there was nothing he could to defuse that. But he also felt totally indecisive. He knew that ultimately he couldn't be friends with Oliver and Ryan at the same time and he felt more comfortable with Ryan. But if he was honest there was something about Oliver's sheer unpredictability that attracted him. He felt partly curious, partly afraid. Was he cycling into a trap?

There was another factor, however, to feed his curiosity – Adam Anlott. Greg had finished *Dream Stealer 5* with considerable relish and had enough allowance to buy *Dream Stealer 6* on the way home. Could Anlott really be Oliver's father, or was Oliver some kind of fantasy merchant? Greg knew he had to find out.

He was cycling through an industrial wasteland with developers' boards everywhere but no sign of development. Everything seemed to have closed – garages, factories, pubs – and there were also rows of boarded-up houses. Because of the dereliction, mass dumping had taken place and the verges and forecourts were littered with old car wrecks and tyres.

He was keeping a look out for The Bantam and eventually spotted the old pub next to an empty carpet warehouse.

Greg got off his bike, feeling decidedly apprehensive, gazing round warily. The sun had come out after an overcast morning and the clouds were rolling away to reveal a blue sky. He could just make out faded lettering on a billboard. THE GRANGE ROLLER-SKATING RINK. FUN FOR ALL. An arrow pointed the way behind the pub and Greg pushed his bike down a refuse-heaped side road to a dome-like one-storey building whose sign once again proclaimed THE GRANGE ROLLER-SKATING RINK. Greg shivered in the darting breeze. It would be far more sensible to go home. But he couldn't. His curiosity was too great, overwhelming his fear. And the excitement of the unpredictable stirred yet again.

The rink had once resembled a one-storey medieval castle with slit windows and false turrets. A rusty steel shutter had been pulled down over the entrance and Greg slowly pushed his bike past the long building towards the car park where tall grass had grown up through broken tarmac.

'Hello, Greg.'

Greg jumped and almost dropped his bike. Oliver's familiar voice seemed to emerge from somewhere below ground. Then Greg saw him looking out of a trap door in the concrete paving, just below the wall of the rink.

'Hello, Greg,' he repeated.

'What are you doing down there?' Greg's voice was bright and artificial.

'This is the way in. It's where they used to deliver booze.'

'Is that the only way in?'

'And out.'

Greg hesitated. The trap had been set. Once he was down there – would he ever escape? Immediately he told himself to stop being stupid.

Slowly he leant his bike against the wall and padlocked the wheel. Then he strolled across to Oliver.

He looked white and strained, with beads of sweat on his forehead. But then it *was* very hot.

'Come on,' said Oliver encouragingly.

'OK.'

'Not scared, are you?'

'Why should I be?'

He glanced down and saw that Oliver was standing on a flight of rickety wooden steps.

'Make sure you close the trap door behind you.'

Then everything will be in darkness, said the warning voice in Greg's mind.

Hesitantly, he reached the first step, climbed down and then stretched up and closed the hatch. There was a faint glow from below and Greg realised it was the pinprick gleam of a torch.

'Is it all dark in here?'

'No. These are the cellars. They go way back.'

'In length?'

'In age.' Oliver sounded impatient. 'There was an old

hotel here before the rink.'

'And now there's just an old rink,' said Greg fatuously.

'Some of the windows aren't boarded up on the other side. So we've got *some* light. Come and meet the guys.'

Guided by Oliver's torch Greg climbed up another flight of steps where a grey light dimly lit some battered lockers, a Wall's ice-cream sign and a long, low counter with a sign saying ROLLER SKATE RENTALS.

Then Greg could see a large circular rink, almost entirely covered in ripped-up seats, a smashed Coca Cola machine, hundreds of crushed cans, loads of broken wooden crates, dismembered bikes and boards advertising old attractions. No one else seemed to be around. Was he alone with Oliver? Greg felt a sense of creeping unease.

The grey light made everything dun-coloured and there was a scampering from behind some benches that he didn't like the sound of.

'We've got rats,' said Oliver casually.

'That's nice.'

'And mice and cockroaches and silverfish and beetles –'

'So you don't get lonely.' Greg was determined not to be wound up. 'Aren't you trespassing?'

'Probably.'

'How long has this place been closed?'

'Years. It's going to be pulled down – but not yet.'

'So what do you use it for? It's a bit gloomy, isn't it?'

'I told you. We built this assault course.'

'Here?' Greg looked round as nonchalantly as he could. The scampering sound came again.

'Next door.'

'So where are your mates?'

'Impatient, aren't you?' Oliver walked alongside the rink and turned left, opening a door that was already half off its hinges.

The Geeks were sprawling across a mass of old cushions in a room that had once been a snack bar. The place smelt bad, partly of sweat and partly of a shut-in dampness. The four boys were not a very prepossessing sight, and although Greg vaguely recognised them from school, he couldn't identify any of them by name.

'Here's the challenger,' said Oliver.

'What?' Greg was instantly alarmed. Had Oliver set him up? Had that been his intention all along?

'You're going to try and beat the record on the assault course.' Oliver sounded as if the plan had already been discussed in some detail.

'Am I?'

'Meet the Geeks,' said Oliver with a certain amount of pride. 'This is Pug.'

There was no question of shaking hands. Pug remained sprawled on the dirty cushions. He had cropped hair and his pasty face was amazingly pug dog like. His bloated-looking body belied the muscles in his arms that stood out like cords from his short-sleeved T-shirt.

'Hi.' Pug gazed up at Greg with pale, washed-out blue eyes.

'Meet Fabian.'

He was even fatter than Pug, but was taller than Oliver. His hair was in dreadlocks which hung beaded down to his shoulders.

'And Hassan.'

He also had dreadlocks, but although they were unbeaded they were even longer, his thin face almost lost amongst his elaborate hairstyle. Once again Greg noticed Hassan's arms were very muscular.

'And Denny.'

He had carefully jelled jet-black hair and his clothes, a coloured shirt and dark trousers with highly polished shoes, were much more expensive and carefully looked after.

'You come to take us on?' asked Hassan.

'Greg's come because he's a mate of mine,' snapped Oliver. 'We've both helped each other out, but I'm not going to say just how and it doesn't matter anyway. And anyone's who's a mate of mine –'

'Is a mate of ours.' Pug had a curiously soft voice and his eyes dwelt on Greg almost clingingly. His scrutiny was unnerving.

Suddenly Greg profoundly wished he had never come. The Sweats were better company any time. They were probably out playing football even now, or at the youth club, not lying around in some filthy tip.

'Where's the assault course?' demanded Greg, wanting to do whatever he had to do and then go. At least, he hoped they'd let him go.

'Let's take a look,' said Oliver and the others got up, surrounding Greg as if he was being taken to the scaffold.

'No need to look so scared,' Pug grinned.

'I'm not.'

'It's easy,' said Hassan.

'No it's not,' snapped Denny.

'It's kind of difficult, I think. Especially if you're scared of heights.' Fabian gazed straight at Oliver, who suddenly looked slightly discomforted.

'I got over that.' Oliver was more subdued now.

'We haven't seen you,' Fabian pointed out.

'OK. I'll prove it. I'll go up with Greg.'

'You'll get in his way,' said Pug. 'He's trying to beat the record.'

Greg had the impression that Oliver was only just in charge. He wondered if he was right, or was the put-down talk only a kind of teasing?

'Whose record is it?' asked Greg uneasily.

'Mine,' said Denny. 'Two minutes, twenty-nine point zero three seconds.' He pulled out an expensive-looking stop-watch.

'I'll time you.'

Then the others pulled out their own stop-watches. They were identical and Greg was sure they'd been stolen. The Geeks grinned.

Greg and the Geeks followed Oliver down a long passage that was almost pitch dark, and Oliver flashed his torch ahead until they came to another door that had been partly kicked in. Greg wondered if the Geeks had done all this damage or if vandals had got into the rink before them.

Ragged light shone from an unboarded window high above and Greg saw they were now in a large room which looked as if it had once been a gym. There was a vaulting horse pushed against the damp-stained wall and the rowing machine looked as if it could still be used.

The assault course had a high ropes section as a centre-piece, with a rope ladder each end. Then there were tyres strung to form a tunnel on the floor, some boards nailed together to make a high scramble wall, a cargo net slung under the high ropes and a set of posts on which the contestants presumably had to balance.

Greg wished he wasn't wearing jeans. They would really slow him up. If only he'd brought some tracksuit bottoms or his football shorts. Anyway, it was too late now.

'You have to do it this way,' said Oliver, gazing up at the high ropes. 'One: you go through the tunnel; two: you climb the wall and drop down; three: you get yourself into the cargo net that side – and down the other; four: you balance on the posts; five: you go up the right-hand ladder, along the high ropes and down the left-hand ladder. OK? Shall I run over it again?'

'I think you'd better,' said Greg. Some of the course looked tricky, particularly the balancing posts and the high ropes, but he was determined to beat Denny.

Oliver ran over the details one more time.

'You ready to start?'

'Why not?' Greg tried to look cool and laid-back, but he was feeling increasingly nervous. It was not so much the course that alarmed him, but the fact that the Geeks were watching. What would happen if he failed to beat Denny's record? Would they send him up? Or would it go much worse if he *did* beat Denny?

TEN

'Are you ready?' asked Oliver.

'As I ever will be,' Greg muttered.

'I'll call out the numbers – *and* the directions.'

'You didn't do that for me,' objected Denny.

'You helped to build the course.' Oliver seemed more in charge now but Greg noticed that Pug was watching Oliver carefully.

Denny shrugged.

Pug checked his new stop-watch.

Hassan gazed at Greg. So did Fabian.

'Are you ready?' asked Oliver again.

Greg nodded.

'On your mark. Set. Go!'

He rushed into action like a spring uncoiled as he caught Denny's tense glance. I'll have you, Greg said to himself.

Greg's heart thumped painfully as he sped towards the tunnel of tyres, hurling himself into it, trying to count the seconds and soon giving up the impossible task. All he could do was to use every ounce of determination he had. He also used his anger, surging through the tunnel, and without hesitating for a moment flinging himself at the wall, pulling with his wrists, scrabbling with his feet until he was on top, jumping down to the other side, skinning one hand as he momentarily failed to keep it clear.

He gave a howl of pain and for an instant gazed back at the huddle of Geeks who were watching him silently. Oliver looked disappointed. Did he want him to win, wondered Greg as he grabbed at the bottom of the net with his torn fingers and then somersaulted backwards into its sagging coils. He rolled over and over to the other side, somehow standing, and then doing another backward somersault out of the net on to the floor, pulling himself up on to one of the posts and then zig-zagging between them, almost slipping, nearly falling, without a word of encouragement from below.

Soon Greg was swarming up the rope ladder and on to the high ropes. He had no fear of heights and managed them easily, stabilising the bridge as he went until he reached the ladder on the other side, diving down to the floor where he collapsed gasping, face down, not wanting to look at any of them, relishing the feeling of being gloriously, wonderfully still.

Pug glanced down at his stop-watch and said quietly, 'Sorry.'

Greg dragged himself to a sitting position. 'What's that?'

'You didn't make it.'

'What was my time.'

'Seven seconds short of Denny's.'

'Let me see.'

But Pug had already clicked the stop-watch back to zero.

'You could have fiddled that.'

'No way,' laughed Denny. 'Pug's as honest as the day.'

Greg thought the comment was ludicrous. Now he was on his feet, turning to Oliver in anger and dismay.

'I saw the time,' said Oliver. 'You blew it. Only just though.' He smiled. 'Want to have another go?'

Was he enjoying torturing him, wondered Greg.

'Now?' Despite his exhaustion, Greg felt a rising anger.

'After a rest.'

'Got any water?'

'I'll find some.'

'OK. I'll try again. Give me ten minutes.'

'We'll give you as long as you like,' said Pug. 'There's no hurry.'

Greg lay propped up against the wall, his anger dying back, turning into a quiet, steely determination, while the others went out, only leaving Pug who seemed to be taking a quiet pleasure in his failure.

'Not good enough,' he said.

'I'll do it next time.'

'You stand even less chance. You're knackered.'

'Go to hell!'

'Watch your lip.'

Greg closed his eyes against the mockery.

'Mate of Oliver's, are you?' asked Pug.

'Sort of.'

'No one's a *real* mate of his.'

'What do you mean?'

'We stick together.'

'I thought Oliver was – the boss.'

Pug grinned again. 'Take me to your leader,' he muttered.

'Well – is he, or isn't he?'

'We take good care of Ollie. Keep him from his true self. Try to see he behaves.'

'Behaves? What are you on about?'

'Ollie's a bit weird.'

'Is – is his dad Adam Anlott?'

Pug shook his head. 'Where did you get that from?'

'Oliver.'

'Well. I did tell you he was a bit weird, didn't I?'

Oliver returned with a bottle of warm water but to Greg it was the most exquisite drink he had ever had.

'You were great, wasn't he, Pug?' said Oliver proudly.

'He certainly was.'

How strange, thought Greg. Now Oliver's back, Pug has resorted to his role as lieutenant again. Maybe Oliver *is* the strongest after all.

'Ryan would never get your timing,' said Oliver. 'There's not a Sweat to beat you.'

'I wouldn't say that.'

'I would.'

'I lost.'

'Denny's had a lot of practice.'

'How long has this course been up?'

'Six months. Maybe more.'

'And Denny's been on it lots?'

'Yes,' said Pug. 'You were amazing. There was only a few seconds in it and you've never even tried the course before.'

Greg looked up at Pug and Oliver. Suddenly he wanted to succeed for them, be accepted. He liked the praise, the sense of achievement, and doing the course was fun.

'I'll clip those seconds off,' said Greg. 'No trouble.'

They both smiled and nodded at him, having faith, as if they were the elders of a tribe and he was a young warrior in training. Amazed by this sudden sense of belonging, Greg got shakily to his feet as Pug pulled out his stop-watch.

'Sure you've had enough rest?'

Greg nodded.

'Want some more water?' asked Oliver.

Greg put the bottle to his lips. 'OK,' he gasped.

Pug set the watch.

Greg was through the tyres as if he was a snake, over the wall like a gazelle, into the net like a monkey, on to the balancing posts like a lemur and over the rope bridge like a chimp. He had never felt so mindless, so instinctive and so animal-like before, hardly noticing the strain, barely remembering the fact that he was trying to break a record.

It was only when Greg crashed to the ground at Oliver and Pug's feet that he felt the sweeping, aching exhaustion. 'How did I do?' he stuttered, the sweat running into his eyes.

'You did well.' Pug spoke slowly. 'You did so well that you broke the record. You clipped four seconds off Denny's time.' He paused for effect. 'So you're the new champion.'

Greg gazed up at them in disbelief and then gave a great whoop of joy. So did Pug and Oliver. They grabbed him, heaved Greg off the ground and staggered around, hugging each other, yelling, until Oliver pushed them apart. 'We're making too much noise.'

As Denny, Fabian and Hassan appeared at the door Pug said, 'He did it!'

Denny looked taken aback, but didn't seem particularly put out, rushing up to Greg and whirling him round.

Then there followed a long, panting, gasping silence which was eventually broken by Oliver as he said proudly, 'You're a Geek, my son.'

Greg gazed at them open-mouthed, the heady, adrenalin-based elation rapidly dying away. What had he been thinking of? He didn't want to be a Geek. That was the last thing he ever, ever wanted to be.

A sudden suspicion swept Greg as he gazed at Pug and his stop-watch. Suppose all this had been the ultimate wind-up? Suppose there never had been any timings or record?

Suppose Denny had never achieved anything? After all, Greg hadn't been allowed to so much as glance at the stop-watch, either on his first or second attempt. Suppose Pug had fixed the time, lied, falsified everything. It was certainly a possibility.

'I don't want to be a Geek,' said Greg slowly.

Pug grinned, Oliver looked away and the others shifted uneasily.

'Oliver said you'd want to be a Geek – particularly if you broke the record,' said Hassan. 'Now you've put all that effort in for nothing.'

Soaked in cold sweat, Greg shook his head. 'It wasn't for nothing.'

'Then what was it for?' demanded Fabian.

'For myself – for the fun of it.'

'That wasn't much fun, was it?' asked Denny.

Oliver walked casually over, raised his hand and slapped Greg hard round the face. Greg staggered back against the wall, staring at Oliver in amazement, feeling a stunning sense of betrayal.

'What did you do that for?' he muttered, tears of pain starting in his eyes.

'You wasted our time.'

'I broke the record.' Greg paused. 'Didn't I?'

Pug looked at the stop-watch again, hugging it close to his chest. 'I could have made a mistake.' He grinned.

'Could you? How?'

'I never was any good with these things.' He grinned again.

'OK,' stuttered Greg. 'OK. It's between you and me, Denny. You go first. We'll re-run the whole damn thing.'

'No way.'

'Why not?'

'Don't fancy it.'

'I'll take on any of you,' yelled Greg. 'But someone else has got to operate that stop-watch.'

'The fun's over,' said Pug.

'There never was any record, was there?' Greg was bitter. 'You just wound me up and made me look a fool. Got me completely knackered for nothing.'

'You said you had fun,' said Pug. 'That was *our* fun.'

Greg suddenly threw himself at Pug and the surprise of the attack took them both to the ground, rolling over and over on the concrete floor. But Greg was far too exhausted to fight and Pug soon had him on his back, kneeling on his arms and spitting in his face.

Pug got off and Oliver went over to help Greg up, but Greg kicked out at him feebly and the others burst into raucous laughter.

Denny looked down at his watch. 'Time passes quickly when you're having fun,' he said quietly. 'Now it's time to go home.'

'The fun hasn't finished,' said Fabian as Greg dragged himself to his feet, aching in every part of his body. 'Oliver hasn't been over the high ropes.'

There was a long silence.

'You said you did it.' Hassan looked at Oliver in rising contempt. 'So why can't you do it again?'

'All right,' said Oliver hesitantly. 'I'll have a go.'

Was this part of some other game, wondered Greg. Then, in spite of his fury, he suddenly wanted to put a stop to all this cruelty, even to protect Oliver from himself.

'You don't have to,' he advised him.

'Shut up!' yelled Oliver. 'You're not a Geek so you've got no right to give an opinion.'

Greg shrugged and sat down again, wondering what would happen next.

Oliver's long, lanky frame swarmed up the rope ladder and on to the first length of the rope bridge. Then he paused and looked down, his eyes glassy, hands trembling.

'I did it before,' he called down.

'We'll believe you when we *see* you do it.' Denny was merciless.

'I do it on my own.'

'Do it with us watching,' yelled Fabian.

Greg felt a surge of pity, and something else. Was it companionship? He suddenly felt as he had when he had been with Sean and Tim and Ryan after the football training. That there was something between them. A bond. Now Oliver seemed to be looking directly down at him and Greg felt the bond tighten. Despite all the problems that Oliver had given him, all the mixed emotions – hostility and aggression and determined possessiveness – Greg wanted him to be safe and do well and reassure his shambolic assortment of Geeks that he was fit to lead them.

'Go on,' said Greg. 'You can do it.'

As if magically transformed, Oliver began to walk steadily and confidently across the rope bridge, correcting its sway, balancing his weight, even smiling a little.

It was only when he was scrambling down the opposite rope ladder that Greg wondered if the game had still been on and that Oliver had tricked him yet again.

Greg gazed at the Geeks as they gave Oliver muted applause, and realised how devious they were. The whole bunch of them must be on a continuous wind-up, not only of him, not only of each other, but of life itself. He pitied them, but he also had to admit he still liked the daring and the risk-taking.

And that was the point, for that was why he found them so compelling. You never knew where you were with a Geek. Greg smiled inwardly. The phrase sounded like a TV commercial. With Ryan and his friends he knew exactly where he was, but with the Geeks nothing was what it seemed, and everything and everyone appeared to have a double meaning. It was like magic – anything could happen – and Greg had no doubt he wanted more, although he was ashamed of how he felt.

He suddenly realised that being a Geek was a continuous challenge. They took risks – and it was risks that Greg wanted because they blocked his mind. He hadn't heard Rachel crying ever since he'd got here and he hadn't felt the least stab of jealousy. The Geeks could blot out the pain that usually went on in his head all the time. They *were* magic – and that's what he needed.

As Oliver reached the ground, Greg clapped him on the back and said, 'Well done. I knew you could do it.'

Oliver didn't get the rough-house pummelling response that Greg had received. The other Geeks stood back, humble and admiring, ready to receive their leader back, as if he had been readmitted into the game.

For the next half-hour, Greg, Oliver and the other Geeks swarmed over the assault course in heady triumph, jumping about on the ropes, trying to push each other off – but no one fell or got hurt.

Greg began to feel that he had entered a special inner circle, that whilst he was with the Geeks he could run enormous risks and nothing would happen. All his annoyance and disgust – even his fight with Pug – was forgotten. The pure physical sensation, the companionship, the continuous excitement, made Greg forget his misery and isolation.

'This is it,' he yelled at Oliver as they both swung down the ropes to the ground. 'This really is it!'

ELEVEN

'Had a good time?' asked Oliver as he and Greg cycled home.

There was a cool breeze, making the heat more bearable, and the tail-wind made the cycling easier. Even the traffic seemed lighter, and despite all his aches and pains, Greg felt wonderfully exhilarated and slightly light-headed.

'I'm sorry about Pug.' Once again, Oliver was playing the role of someone who was older and wiser.

'I was knackered. I could have taken him if –'

'Yes. Yes.' Oliver was briskly adult. 'Pug can get out of control, but he's loyal at heart.'

Greg wasn't so sure about that but he wanted to avoid anything that was controversial. Then, almost as if he was speaking against his will, he heard himself saying, 'Do you think he fiddled the stop-watch?'

'I don't know.' Oliver sounded as if he didn't care much either. 'How's Ryan?' he asked.

'OK.'

'The football fun too?'

'It was OK.'

'Who did you have more fun with?' Oliver's tone was sharp and insistent and a warning bell began to ring in Greg's mind, but he chose to ignore it.

'You lot.'

'Ah.'

Greg turned to glance at Oliver and saw his gaunt face had gone pink with pleasure. The warning bell sounded again.

'Why did you enjoy us so much?'

'I never knew what was going to happen next,' said Greg hesitantly.

'And you know what's going to happen next at football?'

'Sort of.'

'I don't expect you to be a Geek.'

Greg immediately felt alarmed, as if something important was being withdrawn. 'I don't mind.'

'You don't mind what?'

'I don't mind being a Geek.'

'Yes?'

'If you'll have me.' Suddenly Greg was desperately anxious not to be rejected. The Geeks blotted out the pain. He needed them.

'Why not?'

Greg suddenly remembered the Drops. 'But I'm not having anything to do with your war against the Sweats.'

'You've got to come down on one side or the other.'

'Then I won't belong to either.' Greg had suddenly come to his senses, neatly sliding out of the commitment. Had he gone crazy? What had he been going on about magic for?

'It doesn't matter,' said Oliver magnanimously. 'You can be piggy in the middle then.'

Greg didn't reply.

'So at least we'll be mates –'

'Why not?'

'Want to meet my dad then?'

'Er –'

'You don't have to.'

'I'd like to.' Greg suddenly didn't want to miss the opportunity.

'Why not come round my house tomorrow?'

'Won't he be busy writing?'

'Dad can spare you a few minutes. Then we can play on the computer. I'll cook you lunch.'

'You cook as well?'

'I'm good. At least, my dad thinks so.'

'OK.'

They were nearing home now.

'Where do you live?' asked Greg.

Oliver gave him the address and grinned. 'I'm glad we're friends,' he said.

But Greg now felt only a sense of disquiet.

'You had another chum call,' said Dad delightedly as Greg came into the house. 'I knew you'd find your feet.' Then he stared at him in amazement. 'What on earth have you been doing? You're filthy – and you stink.'

'I was – messing about with some mates.'

'In a bog?'

'On an assault course. It was fun. I broke the record.'

'Oh well, it kept you out of mischief, I suppose.'

'Where's Mum?'

'Up with Rachel.' His father looked at him anxiously. 'The poor little thing's not so well. Got a bit of a summer cold.'

'Who phoned?' asked Greg brusquely.

'A chap called Ryan.'

'I'll give him a call.'

'How about a shower first?' Dad began, but Greg was already reaching out for the phone book to look up Ryan's number.

TWELVE

'How did you get on?' asked Ryan. He sounded anxious.

'What with?'

'The Geeks, of course.'

'They were OK.' Greg was deliberately casual.

'What about the assault course?'

'That was OK.'

'So they didn't drop you?'

'No.'

'Want to come over tomorrow? See a match on Sky?'

'I'd love to, but I can't.'

'OK.' Ryan sounded disappointed. 'What did you think of them?'

'The Geeks? They were –'

'OK?' Ryan filled in for him. 'You're not saying much, are you?'

'There's not much *to* say.'

'I had another of those notes. First one to be sent in the post. Lucky my parents didn't open the envelope. I'll read it to you.' He paused. 'Hang on. I'm just going to close the sitting-room door – I don't want anyone to overhear this.'

When he got back, Ryan began to speak in a soft voice. Too soft.

'I can't hear you,' said Greg.

'OK. But I can't talk much louder.' He began to read the note. 'YOU'LL TAKE THE BIG DROP SOON. YOU'RE NOT GOING TO SURVIVE IT.'

'Christ!' said Greg.

'What does he mean by the *Big* Drop?' Ryan's voice broke slightly, and Greg realised the extent of his fear.

'I don't know,' said Greg. 'But you've got to show that to someone.' He was appalled. Could this be Oliver's work? If it was, he *was* mad. But hadn't he known that all along? Suddenly he was in the real world again, looking back on the afternoon as anything but exciting, and the feeling of bonding with Oliver and the Geeks abruptly disappeared. Had *he* gone mad?

'Who can I show it to?' Ryan seemed helpless.

'Your parents?'

'No way. They've got enough problems of their own. They never take any notice of me, except when I'm in trouble. They wouldn't care. They'd think it was a joke.'

'What about Mr James?'

'I'm not showing myself up.'

'So what are you going to do?'

'Sit tight.'

Greg swallowed. 'He doesn't mean it.'

'You should know.' Ryan sounded accusing.

'What do you mean?'

'You consort with him. You know where the Geeks hang

out. Maybe you even saw Oliver writing this note. Did you all have a good laugh?' Ryan's voice rose and then died away to a whisper. 'At my expense.'

'Ryan –'

'Why don't you tell me what's going on?' Ryan demanded threateningly.

'Because I don't know!'

'You must do!'

'I don't know anything about the note. All I did was to go over their stupid assault course. Get yourself together – I'm not in with the Geeks. I don't want to be a Geek.'

'You don't want to be a Sweat either.'

'I want to be my own person. I've told you that.'

'Yes.' Ryan sounded unimpressed.

'You – *we've* got to do something about that note. What about Sean and Tim? Have you told them?'

'Just now –'

'And?'

'They're scared.'

'Aren't you?'

'No.' The lie was obvious.

'Do you want me to come over?'

'I've got to go out with my dad.'

Was this just a tit-for-tat? Greg wasn't sure.

'Give me a ring tomorrow.' Ryan paused. 'Tell me something.'

'If I can.'

'Why does this guy Oliver hate me so much? I mean, even more than Tim and Sean? What have *I* done?'

'You sent him up.' Greg's statement was flat and cold. 'You flushed his pendant down the toilet.'

'It was only a joke.'

Greg said nothing.

'It doesn't warrant making death threats. Isn't that a criminal offence?'

'Probably. Why don't you go to the police?'

'I can handle it.' Ryan didn't sound as if he could.

'I'll help you,' said Greg suddenly.

'How?'

'I'll talk to Oliver. Except we don't know if it *is* Oliver sending you the notes. Do we?'

'It's obviously him. Who else could it be?'

'Some other kid? Another Geek?'

'I don't think so.' Ryan sounded as certain as he was desperate. 'So you're going to see him again?'

Greg paused, knowing what he was about to say was going to go down like a ton of bricks. 'Actually, I'm going to Oliver's house tomorrow.'

'You're what?' Ryan sounded both appalled and betrayed.

'He wants me to meet his father.'

'What for?'

'He says he's Adam Anlott.'

'Bullshit!'

'I thought I'd go and prove it one way or the other.'

'Is that the only reason you're going?' Ryan sounded suspicious.

'Yes.' There was a long pause. 'It can't just be the sending up – maybe he's jealous of you.'

'Why?'

'You're everything he's not. Popular. Good at sport. Good looking. He just looks like a – a –' Words began to fail Greg.

'A Geek?' Ryan tried to laugh but failed.

'You should see them.'

'The other Geeks?'

'They're a weird bunch.'

'Pug – he gives me the creeps. The others are just misfits.'

'Like Oliver?'

'You think that too?' Ryan sounded cheered.

Greg, however, still remembered the happy companion-ship of cycling home with Oliver after such a strange afternoon. He felt he had somehow betrayed them both.

'When are you going to get off that phone?' hissed his father from the sitting-room door.

'I've got to go,' said Greg. 'I'll call tomorrow.'

'You said you were going to talk to the bastard – what are you going to say?' asked Ryan.

'To stop bothering you. To stop being such a prick. That's what I'm going to say.'

Greg lay awake that night, thinking about Ryan and Oliver and his own predicament. He knew Ryan was now terribly afraid, and no wonder after what had happened to Tim and Sean, but surely the note was an obvious wind-up? Despite this, Greg knew he was still drawn to the Geeks' special brand of excitement – and the more he dismissed it as wrong, the more he wanted another dose. With the Sweats he knew where he was. Football, girls, the youth club. OK, he liked football, but he wasn't into girls and had never been to the youth club and didn't particularly want to go anyway. Life with the Geeks was mysterious, eventful, dramatic. And now he had another reason for seeing Oliver, apart from sussing out his father – to protect Ryan and stop him being persecuted in this horrible way. Oliver had gone too far, and although Greg had tried to explain to Ryan *why* Oliver hated him so much, he still wasn't sure what drove Oliver to such extremes. He *had* to find out.

Oliver's house was large and shabby, part of a Victorian terrace that was on the opposite side of the common. As he cycled up, Greg could see Oliver standing on the stone steps, anxiously watching the road.

'I thought you weren't coming.'

'It's only ten. That's the time you said.'

'I still didn't think you were coming.'

'Well, I'm here, aren't I?'

'Come in then.' Oliver looked immensely relieved, as if he had been preparing for disappointment.

★

Once inside, Greg found the house dark and gloomy, with piles of newspapers scattered around, boxes in the corner of the sitting room and shabby furnishings. There were hardly any pictures on the walls, which didn't look as if they had had a coat of paint for a long time.

Then Greg heard the gentle tapping upstairs.

'What's that?' he asked.

'My dad typing,' said Oliver, so softly that Greg could hardly hear him.

'Is he working on another *Dream Stealer*?'

'He doesn't do anything else these days.'

'When can I meet him?'

'Later. I'll have to get permission. He doesn't like being interrupted.'

'OK. What shall we do?' Greg asked rather grumpily.

'Want a go on my computer?'

'All right.'

But Oliver didn't move. 'Actually, I'm compiling a *Dream Stealer* myself. Dad and I are going to write the book together.'

'Will it have your name on?'

Oliver seemed taken aback. 'I don't know.'

'I want to ask you something.' Greg had decided to take advantage of what he thought was a weak moment as far as Oliver was concerned.

'What is it?'

'Get off Ryan's back.'

'I don't get you.' Oliver's face was expressionless.

'Yes, you do. You keep sending him notes in school and now the first one arrived in the post. It was pathetic.'

'I haven't sent him any notes –'

'Yes, you have.'

'Don't shout or my dad will get upset,' Oliver whispered urgently.

'I'm not shouting. You wrote that Ryan was to be hung by the neck until he was dead. You've got to stop.'

'I tell you – I've never written any notes to Ryan.'

'Then who did?'

'Maybe it was Pug – or even one of the others.'

'Don't you *know*?'

'They don't tell me everything.'

Greg hesitated. Could Oliver be telling the truth? He certainly didn't sound as if he was lying. But maybe Oliver was a practised liar. Then a sudden idea came into Greg's mind. The only way he'd know for sure if Oliver was a fantasist or not would be to establish the identity of the man upstairs. And if Oliver wasn't going to introduce them, then Greg would just have to find some other way of seeing him.

'You tell them to stop sending the notes,' Greg warned him.

'I'll try,' said Oliver mildly.

'OK. Let's have a look at your computer then.'

★

Oliver led him into a small, rather poky room that had once been a study. The walls were hung with hessian and there was a desk by the main window. The chintz curtains were firmly drawn against the sun outside.

The floor was stacked with piles of comics, and there were a couple of *Dream Stealers* lying on a shelf that was crammed with more comics, some of them quite babyish.

On the desk was a complicated computer setup and printer, and two sets of games controls.

'Why do you keep all those comics?' asked Greg curiously.

'They're old friends,' replied Oliver defensively.

'It's a nice room.' Greg knew he sounded feeble and insincere. In fact he thought the room was awful, claustrophobic and dark. To be alone with Oliver in this room was particularly creepy.

'It used to be my mother's study. She was in marketing.'

'Where is she now?' asked Greg.

'Dead.'

'Sorry.' He was embarrassed.

'She died a couple of years ago.' Oliver went over to the computer and switched it on. The screen glowed blue and Greg had a sudden, horrifying sensation that the room was deep under the sea and the chintz and hessian were frondy dark weeds in which strange creatures dwelt. The fuggy atmosphere added to the illusion of being trapped in the depths, and for a moment he imagined that he and Oliver were clad in wetsuits with oxygen cylinders on their backs.

'Don't you like the sun?' asked Greg.

'Why?' Oliver seemed confused.

'You've got the curtains drawn.'

'It's where Mum looked out – the same view. I don't want to –' He tailed off and then picked up again. 'There's a cherry tree in the front garden that Mum called her Thinking Tree. She used to look at the tree and get ideas.'

Although Oliver seemed quite open with his confidences, Greg felt a tension building.

'Do you want to play some games?'

'OK.'

But all Greg really wanted to do was open the curtains.

For a while they played a computer game about a space-age attack on London which seemed interminable and which Oliver won easily. Maybe he sits in here and plays these games all day when he's not with the weirdo Geeks in their smelly old rink, thought Greg. Did he ever go outside?

Suddenly, Greg's loyalties swung erratically round again and he wanted to be back on the pitch, football training, running, tackling, kicking the ball. He was getting a splitting headache, particularly when Oliver loaded another game in which the contestants had to race their sports cars over winding mountain roads, through tunnels, negotiating hairpin bends. Greg crashed his car continually. Oliver didn't.

'Let's do something else,' said Greg at last, barely able to control his temper.

'What?' asked Oliver bleakly.

'Let's see your *Dream Stealer*.'

Oliver looked doubtful.

'I'd like to read it.'

'I haven't done much.'

'Can't we see it on the screen?'

Oliver unloaded the game and switched disks, tapped a few times on the keyboard, and the title *DREAM STEALER* 7 came up on the screen.

'You're not going to like this,' said Oliver.

'Why not?'

He didn't answer directly, but merely said, 'It's only my fun.'

DREAM STEALER 7
Taking The Drop

Ryan Banks woke up screaming. He had dreamt what fate had in store for him. As his head was thrust into the noose he began to beg for mercy. But there could be no mercy, for the Stealer had reached into his unconscious mind and made his dream the grimmest reality of his pathetic life.

A long silence followed.

'That's awful,' said Greg, shocked and not knowing what to think.

'Do you think it's any good?' asked Oliver naively.

'I think it's awful.'

'Thanks a lot.' Oliver was immediately hostile and the coils of tension tightened.

'You can't put that in a book,' said Greg.

'Why not? It's made up.'

'No, it's not.'

'Ryan hasn't taken the Drop.'

'Tim and Sean did.'

'Those were reprisals,' said Oliver calmly. 'Also a bit of a joke.'

'They might be reprisals,' replied Greg, 'but they were no joke.' He paused. 'You *did* send Ryan that note, didn't you?'

'I didn't.'

'You're sick.'

Greg got up, leaving Oliver staring into the monitor, his long, beaky features shadowy in the half-light.

'Really sick,' Greg repeated, and began to pace about, knocking into a pile of comics and scattering them over the floor. He didn't attempt to try and pick them up, despite Oliver's complaints.

Oliver's mood, however, seemed to lighten. 'Obviously I'm going to change the name in the book,' he said mildly.

'Anyway, that writing isn't up to your – to Anlott's standards.'

'No?' Oliver got to his feet slowly, his face contorted, and for the first time Greg was afraid.

But suddenly Oliver was staring down at the screen, tapping keys and then hitting them harder.

'What's the matter?'

'Something's gone wrong with this thing.'

'What?'

'I've lost some material. There was more I wanted to show you.'

'I don't *want* to read any more of that crap,' muttered Greg, but Oliver didn't seem to hear him, viciously punching at the keys.

'It's gone.'

Greg hovered, saying nothing.

'Why don't you get us some coke? I've got to think this out,' snapped Oliver.

'How much have you lost?'

'Does it bloody matter? Get the coke. I've got to fix this somehow.'

'Where is it?'

'In the kitchen.'

'Where in the kitchen?'

'In the fridge. Where do you think? In the oven?' Oliver's voice rose, but he clapped his hand over his mouth, staring up at the ceiling.

The silence was broken by the tap-tap-tapping of the typewriter upstairs, and in a flash Greg knew this was the moment he'd been waiting for.

THIRTEEN

'How long are you going to be?' asked Greg. His plan was to creep up the stairs and try to get a sighting of Anlott.

'As long as it takes.' Oliver was hardly listening, his hands running over the keyboard, staring ahead, his expression blank.

Suddenly Greg realised he'd never seen a photograph of Adam Anlott. There wasn't one on the paperbacks he'd bought. So how was he going to recognise him? Then Greg remembered seeing a hardback in a bookshop. He was sure that had had a photograph, but he couldn't remember what it had looked like.

'Am I likely to meet your dad?'

'Mm?'

'I said, am I likely to meet your dad today?'

'We'll see. Later, maybe.'

Greg's parents often spoke to him like that, using those very words.

'I'll get the coke.'

Oliver didn't reply.

Greg sauntered out of the room with rather over-stated casualness. Then, in an alcove in the hall, he spotted a couple of hardbacks. Could they be *Dream Stealers*?

Furtively, he grabbed one and turned the book over. As he did so Greg was conscious all the time of the tapping of the typewriter keys upstairs.

The photograph showed a tall man with dark hair and glasses, his face round, with a black beard and pronounced black eyebrows. His eyes were small and he wore an ear-ring in his right ear. Adam Anlott bore no resemblance to Oliver whatsoever, so what was Greg going to gain by creeping up the stairs and spying?

Then Greg cursed himself for being a raving idiot. Of course, if Adam Anlott was typing away upstairs, he was very likely to be Oliver's father. What was the matter with him? But Greg knew what the matter was. He was scared.

Greg began to walk very slowly and as softly as he could up the stairs. All he wanted to do was take a rapid glance at whoever who was up there and then come down again. If he was caught, he would say he was looking for a toilet.

The stairs didn't creak, but Greg kept on thinking they were going to and his mouth was so dry, his heart hammering so hard, that for a moment he thought he was going to pass out. What would happen if Oliver came out and saw him? Or the person upstairs decided to come down? Panic swept Greg and he paused halfway up, unable to decide what to do.

Then he began to climb again, cold and shivering, wishing he'd never embarked on this stupid idea in the first place. Greg had nearly reached the landing and the typing was louder. He heard someone clear their throat, and then there was a muttering under the breath and a sigh. But the tapping never stopped.

He crept on to the landing and guessed that the typing must be coming from a door that opened inwards to a room with whitewashed walls. But that's all he could see, for his view was blocked. To get a glimpse of the typist, Greg realised he would have to peer round the door, which would mean he might be seen, but he felt compelled to continue.

The corridor, like the rest of the house, was piled high with old newspapers but also contained stacks of books, some of which were copies of *Dream Stealers*.

Greg tiptoed down as carefully as he could and arrived at the door so dry-mouthed that he felt his tongue was stuck to the back of his throat. Then he risked a glimpse inside. In direct contrast to the rest of the house, the room was neat and bare with only a desk occupying most of the space.

The man behind the desk was facing the door. Although he looked slightly older than the photograph on the back of the books, he was definitely the same man. The black hair, now slightly receding; the black beard, a little more unkempt. He was tall, bowed over an old-fashioned electric typewriter. Oliver had not been lying. Oliver had been telling the exact truth all the time. Adam Anlott *was* his father. Slowly, just avoiding tripping over a pile of newspapers, Greg began to steal away. As he trod carefully down the stairs, Greg realised that if this was true then so were Oliver's other claims, and his threats to Ryan in particular. Greg shivered. Oliver was even more dangerous than he had thought.

'Any luck?' asked Greg as he came back into the fuggy room.

Oliver didn't reply, still bent over the computer, not touching anything now, just staring deep into the screen. Suddenly he wheeled round. 'Where's the coke then?'

Too late, Greg realised he had forgotten all about it. 'Coke?'

'You went out to get it. Remember?' Oliver was at his most hostile.

'I forgot.'

'So what were you doing?'

'Er?'

'*What* were you doing?' Oliver rapped out.

'Reading *Dream Stealer 2*. I found a copy of the hardback in the hall.'

'Are you mad?'

You shouldn't be asking *me* that question, thought Greg, his panic growing. 'I got really engrossed in it. I'll go and get the coke now. Sorry. How are you getting on? Any luck?' Greg's words were a gabble.

'I lost the stuff.'

'That can happen if you don't save it regularly.'

'Rubbish. I've been thinking about what you said.'

'Yes?'

'Writing about Ryan. I'll write about who I like. When I like. Get it?' His childish rage was both pathetic and unsettling.

'You shouldn't –'

'You don't tell me what to do. Who are you? Who's Ryan? I'll tell you – you're nobodies who don't understand a thing.'

'What are you on about?'

'You don't understand.'

'Understand what?'

'How the world is. You don't allow for anyone who isn't like yourselves.'

'I'm not a Sweat,' said Greg indignantly.

'You're as good as one.'

'I'm different. Like you.'

'What do you mean, I'm different?' Oliver was staring at him intently.

'Well, you don't like the same stuff as the Sweats. Neither do I.'

'You like football.'

'OK. But that's where it ends. They go about in a crowd. I don't like a crowd.' Greg realised that for the first time he had clarified exactly how he felt – to himself as well as Oliver.

'What else don't you like?'

'People thinking the same.'

'Thinking what?' asked Oliver relentlessly.

'For God's sake stop asking questions.'

'I've got one more. And you've got to give me a truthful answer.'

'What is it then?' Greg was wary and reluctant.

'You promise you'll tell me the truth?'

'How can I do that when I don't know the question?'

There was a short silence. Then a look of determination came into Oliver's eyes. He came very close to Greg who could suddenly smell his sour breath.

'Tell me who I am.'

'What?'

Oliver grabbed Greg's arm and began to shake it. 'You've got to tell me who I am!'

What was he on about? Greg was afraid. Was Oliver finally losing it?

'I don't understand.'

Oliver let Greg's arm go and raised his hand as if to slap him as he had done at the rink.

'You hit me,' said Greg, 'and I'll kill you.' He was surprised by his own ferocity and tried to tone it down. 'I'll beat you up.' Now he sounded lame.

Oliver lowered his hand and the glazed look went out of his eyes. 'Sorry about that,' he said chattily, as if he had spilt something.

'That's OK.' Greg was as artificial as he was.

'Would you like some lunch?'

'Maybe I should be going.'

'Oh, don't go. Have some lunch. I'm a good cook. I'm afraid my father will be too busy to see you today. Another time perhaps.'

Was Oliver simply keeping him on a string, Greg wondered, or had he somehow guessed what had happened – or even spied on him? How ludicrous. Had he been spying on Adam Anlott while Oliver had been spying on him?

Greg felt a wave of hysteria and wanted to laugh and cry at the same time. Then he tried to pull himself together. 'What a shame,' he said.

'If he's still typing at this hour, I know he can't be disturbed.' Oliver was glancing down at his watch.

'I'm sorry you lost your stuff.'

'I can always type it out again. I've got a memory like a horse, or is it an elephant?' Oliver laughed awkwardly and then led the way into the kitchen, still talking too glibly and making Greg feel uncomfortable. 'I'm a dab hand at corned-beef hash. Would you like some?'

'Yes please,' said Greg placatingly.

He sat at the kitchen table and watched Oliver prepare the meal. They were both silent.

Once again, Greg felt like a child with Oliver the adult, and yet, only a few minutes ago, the roles had seemed reversed.

Tell me who I am. Tell me who I am. Oliver's voice rang in Greg's ears. How could he have answered a question like that? It was impossible.

Greg watched Oliver deftly stirring the pot, laying out plates, one on a tray.

'Does your dad have his upstairs then?'

'Oh yes.' Oliver was brisk.

'When do you eat together?'

'In the evening.' Oliver sounded defensive and Greg was sure he was lying.

'Can I help?'

'I'm fine.'

'Can I take the tray up to your dad?'

'You wouldn't know the way.'

'He's upstairs, isn't he?'

'How do you know?'

'I can still hear the typewriter tapping away.'

Now they were both playing games again.

'But you wouldn't know where to go when you got to the top of the stairs, would you? Would you?'

Oliver was slicing white bread with a long knife that looked very sharp. He sliced carefully, with great precision, the bread falling perfectly into even pieces. He was looking up at Greg now with a slight smile. It wasn't a pleasant smile. He had stopped slicing.

'You could always tell me where to go.'

'I could – but I won't.'

'I'd just like to help.'

'Dad wouldn't like that. He never wants his writing interrupted.'

'You'd interrupt him.'

'He's used to me.'

'Are you *really* going to write a book together?'

'Of course.' Oliver's hand shook slightly and he put down the knife. He seemed disconcerted again. 'Why shouldn't we?'

The lunch was delicious but eaten in silence after Oliver had taken the tray up to his father. Afterwards he opened a tin of peaches, but only spooned out portions into two bowls.

'Doesn't your dad like peaches?'

'He only likes savoury things. What shall we do this afternoon?'

'I've got to go.'

'Football practice?'

'I'm going out with my dad.'

'That's nice.' Oliver seemed genuinely moved. 'What are you going to do?'

'Swim,' Greg lied, desperate to get out of the house. He knew he had to be careful here. It would be bad luck if Oliver decided to go to the pool too. More than bad luck.

'Do you like swimming?' he asked Oliver.

'Hate it.'

'I was going to ask you to come along.' This next lie, Greg told himself, was all part of the game and, in that sense, was completely justified.

'I can't swim.'

'Not much point then.'

'Do you often go with your dad?'

'Yes.'

'Do you have brothers and sisters?' Oliver was showing an interest in him he had never shown before, but Greg found this as claustrophobic as the room in which they had spent the morning. He must get out – into the sunshine – where he could breathe fresh air.

'No.'

'So you're an only child, like me?'

'That's right.' But although he had no intention of acknowledging Rachel as a sister, Greg didn't want to be 'like' Oliver either. He wanted to distance himself from someone who acted like a vampire, sucking the life-blood out of him – or so it seemed. Greg hadn't thought about Oliver this way before, but now it seemed the perfect description. 'Well.' Greg got to his feet. 'I'd better go.'

'When will I see you again?'

'At school.' Greg felt cornered.

'It's half term soon. Why don't you come down the rink?' Oliver was expansive.

'I might drop in –'

'When?' Oliver asked sharply.

'Can't say.'

'The others liked you.'

'Good.' Greg began to move into the hall. As he headed towards the front door, there was the sound of steps on the landing above them.

'For Christ's sake!' said a voice that was deep and threatening. 'What *is* this muck?'

'Corned-beef hash, Dad.' Oliver was instantly weak and submissive.

'It's terrible stuff. Stinks to high heaven and quite inedible. Take it away.'

'I'll get you something else.' Oliver was immediately placating.

'I'll have some cheese and pickle sandwiches.'

'OK, Dad.'

Oliver and Greg gazed at each other in a mixture of shock and embarrassment. Suddenly Greg felt really sorry for him.

'I'll ring,' he said. 'I'll ring tomorrow. Fix up a date and do something.'

He found it almost agonising when Oliver's face lit up with pleasure and relief. 'Will you?'

'I promise.' Greg opened the front door and the sunlight flooded in.

FOURTEEN

Greg and Ryan were standing on the edge of the diving pool at the local swimming baths, watching a girl run along the springboard and execute a perfect swallow dive into the chlorine-filled water.

After the morning spent cooped up at Oliver's, Greg had decided that going swimming wasn't actually a bad idea. Oliver hated swimming, so Greg would be safe from him at the pool, and some physical exercise would help to clear his head. He also wanted to fill Ryan in on what had happened, so he'd rung him and arranged to meet up.

'So how's Oliver?' Ryan asked, too casually.

'Weird.'

'What's new?'

'I've got a surprise for you.' Greg was pleased that he was able to break into Ryan's complacency. He deserved a shock, Greg felt, although he didn't really know why.

'What's that?'

'Adam Anlott *is* Oliver's father.'

'*What?*' Ryan swung round, looking incredulous. 'Don't give me that –'

'I'm not.'

'How do you know?'

'Something went wrong with Oliver's computer, and

while he was trying to fix it I sneaked off upstairs and took a look at this guy pounding on a typewriter. It was him. Anlott. I saw his photo on the back of a *Dream Stealer*. There couldn't be any doubt about it.'

'I see.' Ryan sounded bleak.

'So Oliver's not such a bullshitter.'

Ryan looked worried. 'Did you find out who sent the notes?'

'Oliver says it wasn't him. We had a row.'

'Do you believe him?'

'I don't know what to believe,' said Greg. 'Not after his father turning out to be Anlott. And there's something else.'

'What?'

'Oliver went all nutty on me. Kept asking me to tell him who he was.'

'There you are –' began Ryan with satisfaction.

'Then his dad told him he couldn't eat what he'd cooked. Said it was rubbish.'

'Was it?'

'No – it was good.'

'Sounds like you had a busy morning.' Ryan yawned in a fake sort of way. 'Don't you think we're making too much of this Geek business? They're a pathetic bunch of losers – that's all.' But Greg knew how afraid he really was.

'You were dead worried about those notes,' Greg pointed out, but Ryan was determinedly brisk about it all, trying to dismiss the threat.

'I was a fool, wasn't I? Come on, let's go and dive. Maybe that girl –'

'Wait a minute.' For some reason Greg felt a threatening presence. It was an extraordinary feeling, almost as if he had suddenly been touched by something cold and wet and reptilian.

Greg gazed around the pool until his eyes rested on the balcony above them where spectators sat, watching the watery mêlée below.

Greg stared up and kept on staring.

'What is it?' demanded Ryan. 'Seen someone you fancy?'

'Not exactly.'

'What is it then?'

'Take a look yourself. There – up in the spectator seats.'

Ryan's eyes swept the balcony, and he went pale. 'I don't believe it,' he muttered, the goosebumps beginning to come up on his arms. 'I just don't believe it.'

Oliver, Pug, Fabian, Hassan and Denny were slumped on the front benches, their feet up on the safety rail.

Oliver gave a friendly wave which Ryan and Greg were quite unable to return.

'What are we going to do?' stuttered Ryan. All his attempted dismissal of the danger had gone and he looked like a frightened nine-year-old.

'Nothing.'

'They're watching us.'

'Of course they are.' Greg was just as shocked, but he was determined to keep calm.

'What *are* we going to do?' Ryan repeated in desperation, beads of perspiration standing out on his forehead.

'Nothing,' Greg repeated.

'How did Oliver know we were here?'

'I told him I was going swimming with my dad this afternoon. Just to get away from him.'

'So?'

'There's only one pool we *could* have gone to and it's this one.'

'So what's he doing?'

'Checking out my story.'

'And now?'

'He's found out I was lying.'

'But what does it matter if we go swimming?'

'To Oliver – a lot.'

'What's he going to do?'

'I don't know.' Greg now felt a creeping fear himself. Oliver's intensity was like a freezing cold spotlight, playing over them both. 'We should carry on as normal. Do some diving.'

'What's normal?' muttered Ryan. 'I'm beginning to forget.'

Rather half-heartedly, Ryan and Greg began to dive, all

too well aware of the scrutiny from the spectator stands. But both were still determined to pretend that they hadn't noticed the Geeks and were, up to a point, successful until Greg mistimed a dive and did a gigantic belly flop.

His mistake was greeted by distant cat-calls and clapping from the gallery but he and Ryan just managed to determinedly ignore their mocking audience.

They continued to dive until they both got cold. Still avoiding the overwhelming temptation to look up they walked casually back towards the changing rooms. It was a pity that Ryan only just saved himself from slipping on the side of the pool, a near-accident that was once again greeted by cheers, clapping and the occasional wolf-whistle.

'Are they going to be hanging around when we get out?' asked Ryan as they got changed.

'So what if they are?' Greg felt emotionally battered but was still resilient. 'Let them do what they like. They'll soon get fed up.' But would they, he wondered.

'I'm going up to the park to meet Sean and Tim. Do you want to come?' said Ryan. He obviously wanted them to leave together for safety.

'What are you going to do?'

'Kick a ball around. If you come we could play two-a-side.'

Greg considered the invitation. The last thing he wanted was to go home and brood over the day's events. It would be good to kick a ball, to get physically rather than mentally tired.

'Yeah – I'd like to come.' He paused. 'Suppose the Geeks *are* waiting for us outside?'

'They'd be no match for us.' Ryan's bravado was hollow. Then, as they left the changing room, he asked, 'You going to see Oliver again?'

'No way.'

'Sure?'

'I can't be bothered.' But even as he spoke, Greg felt a twinge of disloyalty and remembered Oliver's look of pain when his father had been so angry about his lunch.

There had been no sign of the Geeks outside the pool and Ryan and Greg's tension had eased.

When they reached the park and met up with Sean and Tim, the late afternoon sun was boiling hot and the game of football exhausted all four of them. Stripping off their shirts, they lay gasping on the brown grass, too exhausted to go and buy a drink at the little cafe by the entrance to the park.

Ryan began to tell Tim and Sean what had happened at the pool and then recounted some of Greg's experiences that morning – in particular, how Adam Anlott had turned out to be Oliver's father after all.

'That's amazing,' said Tim unhappily. 'I was so sure he was lying.'

'Maybe he still is,' suggested Sean hopefully. 'Maybe

Anlott just rents a room in the house and –'

Greg didn't want the bother of getting up and going to the cafe despite the fact he was desperately thirsty. Instead, he began to fantasise about ice-cold drinks, remembering the lemonade Mum used to make at home, as he still called Swanage. He could see her in his mind's eye now, walking down the summer garden towards him, bearing a tray of ice-cold lemonade in a jug, and frosted glasses.

She knelt down beside Greg as he lay on the warm grass and he could hear the lumps of ice and the lemonade clunking into his glass.

'There you are, lazybones,' she said. 'Try some of that.'

'Greg!' a voice hissed.

'Mm?'

'Look who's coming,' whispered Ryan.

Greg sat up, confused, wanting Mum to come strolling over the grass towards him. Instead, Greg saw Oliver and the Geeks.

'What the hell do they want?' asked Tim.

'We're four against five,' said Sean. 'But we can take 'em all right. No bother. No trouble.' But they knew he was only trying to reassure himself.

Meanwhile, Oliver and the Geeks were striding purposefully towards them, coming to a halt just a couple of metres away.

'What do you want?' asked Ryan.

'I want Greg,' said Oliver. He stepped forward, arms hanging loosely by his sides.

'Where did you get to?' Greg looked up at him. 'I saw you watching us at the pool. Why didn't you speak to us then?'

'It wasn't the right place,' said Oliver deliberately.

Greg got slowly to his feet. His fatigue had redoubled, but he knew he had to take the responsibility. His mother and the lemonade seemed light years away now. Like Swanage. Like love.

'Liar!' spat out Oliver.

'I don't get you.' But of course he did.

'Bloody liar.' Oliver moved closer.

'What are you on about?'

'You said you were going swimming with your dad.' A little pulse beat in Oliver's temple which the other Geeks looked at curiously. Greg suddenly realised they were as uneasy as the Sweats.

'Push off!' said Sean.

'Make me,' replied Oliver.

'We've slapped you lot around before,' Tim warned him. 'Do you want some more?'

'Yeah, and we dropped you! We've been in training,' said Pug. 'It's going to be different now.'

'Let's try.'

'No!' Oliver was imperious. 'This is between me and Greg. Nobody else. So why did you lie to me?' he asked.

'I'm not responsible to you for what I do with my spare

time,' snapped Greg. 'Why don't you push off?'

'You said you were going swimming with your dad,' Oliver repeated.

'He's sick.' The feeble lie was out and Greg wished he hadn't made it. Why should he make excuses to Oliver?

'So you phoned Ryan.'

'Why not?'

Oliver made a rush at him, fists flying, and Greg was taken by surprise, receiving a stinging blow to his cheek and then his chin. He hit back, missed, and they closed, trying to throw each other on to the grass. Again Greg was surprised by Oliver's strength. He struggled to get free until he was tripped and they both fell, kicking and rolling, hitting out at each other and then rolling again.

The fight was watched silently and unenthusiastically by Ryan, Tim and Sean. They didn't call out for Greg and nor did the Geeks call for Oliver.

Gradually, they formed a ring round the struggling, cursing combatants as they rolled about on the grass, first one on top and then the other, parrying blows, sometimes making a strike, grunting and groaning, rolling again until the fight seemed interminable.

Then Oliver sunk his teeth into Greg's ear and he screamed with pain.

'Right – that's enough!' yelled Ryan, and he kicked out at Oliver, catching him in the stomach. He rolled off Greg with a howl.

'You bastard!' Greg was holding his ear which was bleeding and hurting badly.

Oliver was kneeling on the grass, holding his stomach and gasping. Oddly enough not one of the Geeks tried to intervene, to have a go at the Sweats, to do anything but stare down at Greg holding his bleeding ear and Oliver trying to breathe.

Slowly, like a phoenix rising from the ashes, Oliver got to his feet, still clasping his stomach, turning to Ryan, his face working. 'I'll kill you!' he choked.

'I thought you were trying to kill Greg,' Ryan replied.

'He lied to me. He's your shadow, isn't he?'

'Sure.' Ryan's voice was dry.

'He does everything you say.'

'I'd be so lucky.' Ryan grinned. 'Come near me and I'll break your legs. You OK, Greg?'

The blood was dripping from his ear, but apart from the physical pain, Greg was emotionally numb. The shock had been so great that he felt sealed in, oblivious to what was happening.

'I'm OK,' he muttered.

'Fancy biting his ear,' sneered Ryan. 'You're a pathetic creep, aren't you? What's wrong – you sick in the head? You're like a bloody animal.'

With a wild and ferocious cry, living up to Ryan's insult, Oliver ran at him with flailing fists, just as he had done to

Greg. But before he could make contact, at a signal from Pug, Denny and Fabian leapt forward and pinned Oliver's arms up behind his back. He kicked out at them and continued to struggle, but they just managed to hold on to him.

'It's you I'm after,' he yelled at Ryan. 'It won't be long now.'

'What's that supposed to mean?'

'Before you take the Drop. The Big Drop, I mean.'

'So you *did* write the notes. It's you who's the liar. You swore to Greg you didn't.'

'That's just part of my strategy,' said Oliver more quietly.

'Why bother about the Drop?' demanded Ryan. 'Why don't you and I sort things out? If you don't mind waiting for me to go and get an ear shield that is.'

'No,' said Oliver. 'There's been enough violence.' Fabian and Denny let him go and he stood on his own, a weird smile on his lips. Then he turned to stare down at Greg. 'I'm sorry,' he said. 'I lost my temper.'

'I never want to see you again. So why don't you push off!' shouted Greg with utter loathing. 'You're crazy.'

For a moment Oliver looked as if he was about to cry. Then he pulled himself together. 'We can still be friends,' he pleaded.

There was an incredulous silence.

Then Ryan said, 'You are mad, aren't you, Oliver? What are you? You're mad!'

Suddenly Oliver ran at him again, his mouth slightly open, fist raised, a look of manic hatred on his face. This time the Geeks made no attempt to intervene.

Ryan stood back a little, waiting for Oliver to reach him. Then he pulled back his own fist and hit him so hard in the mouth that the blood came in a great spout.

Oliver's hand went to his lip and he muttered thickly, 'You've knocked a tooth out.' He seemed surprised and oddly calm.

'I'll knock out some more if you like,' Ryan told him, while Greg staggered to his feet and limped over, getting between them.

'This has got to stop,' he said. 'It's way out of control. If we – if we don't stop, someone could get really badly hurt.'

'That's right,' said Pug, and Greg wheeled round, surprised at support from such an unlikely source.

'Correction,' muttered Oliver, dabbing at his bleeding mouth, holding the tooth in his other hand and gazing down at it incredulously. 'Someone's going to *die*. But not quite yet. Not today.'

The Sweats and the Geeks stared at each other as if Oliver's threat had been a revelation. Ryan gave a little gasp.

Greg was overtaken by a feeling of hurtling hopelessness, as if there would never be any way out. A course had been set, he told himself, and there was nothing that could be done.

The Geeks looked as anxious as the Sweats. Only Oliver was determined, once more dominating them all. Even now, after all that had happened, he seemed full of a dreadful confidence again.

'You're a nutter,' said Ryan uneasily. 'You ought to be shut up somewhere.'

'I'm shut up at home,' replied Oliver and Greg realised he was right.

'It's the nut-house you should be in.'

'That's where they'll put me,' Oliver said, 'when I've finished with you.' He turned away and began to stride back across the park and the Geeks slowly followed, not attempting to catch him up.

A battle's been fought but no one's won, thought Greg miserably, feeling the pain in his ear and wondering about Oliver's missing tooth. He knew that when he arrived home, his parents would make a fuss about his injury, and although Greg wouldn't tell them how it had been caused they would look after him. They would love him. But what about Oliver? Would his father care about his missing tooth? Greg didn't think so.

Then with a terrible jolt he remembered Rachel. How could he have forgotten her? Would Dad and Mum really give a damn about his ear? Then Greg remembered that Rachel had a cold. She'd been getting all the attention at home while he was ignored. And now it was even worse. Weren't he and Oliver outcasts together?

Tell me who I am, said Oliver in Greg's mind. His ear was throbbing badly.

'He's a right nutter,' repeated Ryan. 'Look what he did to you.'

Greg nodded, but didn't say anything, for he knew Ryan was really wondering what Oliver was going to do to him. Sean and Tim still said nothing.

'What are we going to do?' asked Ryan. 'What am *I* going to do?' He sounded helpless and, to Greg, the question didn't seem very far away from Oliver's '*tell me who I am*'. They were all frightening each other to death and, worse still, the situation was completely out of control.

Oliver had gone right over the top and become completely obsessed with hatred. Greg remembered reading about the two boys who killed a large number of their class mates in a school in America. Those boys had been against Sweats too, except they called them Jocks. But they were the same. Sportsmen, conformists. The socially acceptable. The socially able.

'You'll have to be careful,' said Greg, wishing the others would be more supportive of Ryan. Were they just as scared? Or when it came to the crunch, how much did they really care? He had to tell Ryan he wasn't on his own.

'Be careful?' breathed Ryan. 'How can I?'

'He'll calm down,' said Sean in a belated attempt at reassurance.

'Oh yes,' Tim was too quick to follow. 'He'll calm down all right.'

But Ryan simply looked away, staring across the park, although Oliver and the Geeks had long since disappeared through the gates.

★

Greg knew he couldn't leave things like this, knew that neither Oliver nor Ryan was able to cope. To ignore the situation wouldn't make it go away. He had to take the initiative, despite his still throbbing ear.

When Greg had left the Sweats, and was sure he was out of sight, he hurried into the nearest phone box and called Directory Enquiries. He got Oliver's number, and began to dial, although he wasn't sure whether Oliver would have got home yet.

The phone rang and rang and Greg was about to put it down when a small, dull voice said, 'Oliver Cole.'

'It's Greg.'

'What do you want?' He sounded drained of emotion, even of hatred.

'I wanted to know how your tooth is.' To Greg, his question sounded idiotic.

'It's out,' said Oliver flatly.

'Yes – but –'

'What have you phoned for?' His voice was still dull. There was no sign of hostility. 'Or would you like to speak to my tooth?'

Greg didn't feel like laughing. 'OK, I did lie to you.'

'That's because you loathe me.' His voice shook. 'Like my father does.'

'Do you want me to come round?'

'No.'

'Do you want to keep talking?'

'What about?'

'I'm sure your father doesn't loathe you.'

'How would *you* know? You've never even clapped eyes on him.'

Suddenly Greg had a wild desire to be honest, however destructive it might be. 'Actually –'

'I hate people who say actually. It always means they're going to load stuff on me.'

'Actually I sneaked up the stairs and took a look at your dad.'

'Did you?' Oliver sounded surprised rather than angry. 'And you got away with it?'

'He didn't see me.'

'Why did you do that?'

'I took a look at the back cover of one of the *Dream Stealers* and checked out the photo. Then I – I identified him – in the flesh.'

'Why didn't you tell me? Did you think I was some kind of fantasy merchant?'

'No. Yes. I didn't –' Now Greg was thrown into confusion, instinctively knowing he shouldn't have told Oliver what he had done, sure he had made the situation worse.

'Did you think I was mad?'

Greg was silent.

'Ryan told you that, didn't he?'

'No.'

'Come on. Stop lying. It's second nature for you to lie, isn't it, Greg? That's why we had that fight. That's why I bit your ear. I'll tell you something – I wasn't a violent person before all this started. I was a pacifist.'

'You said you'd trained yourself to be tough,' Greg prompted.

'You bet. The weak don't inherit the earth, do they? Only the strong.'

'Rubbish!'

'You know it's true.'

'Hang on – the money's running out –'

'Don't bother to put any more in.'

'Please, Oliver. Don't let's stop talking. Not now.' Greg rummaged frantically in his pocket and produced some coins, ramming them into the slot. 'You still there?'

There was silence.

'Come on. Are you still there?'

'Yes.'

Greg breathed a sigh of relief as Oliver returned to his obsession.

'Ryan's one of the strong ones, isn't he? Naturally strong. I made myself tough. I had to – because I didn't know who I was, did I? I mean – *you* couldn't tell me, could you?' Oliver was beginning to gabble, and there was the hysterical edge to his voice that Greg had heard before.

He knew he had to calm him down. 'Let me come round.'

'I won't let you in.'

'Please –'

'I've got to cook my father's supper. This is my father's house.'

'You're really terrifying him.'

'My father?'

'Ryan.'

'Good.' Oliver sounded genuinely pleased.

'You've got to stop. Why did you tell me you hadn't written those notes when you had?'

'That makes us both liars.'

'Ryan's scared.'

'I've hardly started.'

'Why do you hate him so much?'

'He rules the earth. He can walk on the face of the planet. I can't.'

'For God's sake –'

'God? He's dead. He died a long time ago. I'm a street fighter, Greg. Did you know that? Now the weak *shall* inherit the earth.'

'You're not weak.'

'I was.'

'You're sick.'

'What?' There was a sudden steely note to Oliver's voice and Greg bitterly regretted being so clumsy, but it was too late now. He had blundered badly.

'You're not well.'

'Are you saying I'm stark, staring, raving mad?'

'No. You're stressed out.'

'Don't patronise me, Greg.'

'We're friends. I can – say what I like,' he said falteringly.

'You can't. We're not friends.'

'We were.'

'You don't know me.'

'I was trying to.'

Oliver paused and then said, 'Get this into your thick head. I never want to see you again. I despise you. You're a Sweat.'

'No.'

'You're a Sweat,' Oliver taunted him. 'You'll always be a Sweat.'

'I'm me.' Greg was almost in tears.

'You're a natural Sweat. I'm a street fighter. Good night.' He crashed down the phone, leaving Greg sure that Oliver was going to do something terrible. He had never felt so afraid in his life.

When Greg reached home the place was in darkness and a sudden, new wave of panic swept him. Opening the front door, he switched on the hall light and immediately saw the note in his father's handwriting on the table. Greg ran towards it, full of dread.

We've had to take Rachel to hospital. She's got pneumonia.

Can you cope on your own for a bit? I'll call as soon as we've spoken to the doctor. Love, Dad.

Greg's mind reeled. How many more shocks could he take? He could hardly believe what he had just read. Then the telephone began to ring. Was it Dad? Or Oliver? He ran to pick up the receiver, knocking a bowl of flowers on to the floor, the water soaking into the carpet.

'Yes?'

'It's Dad. You saw my note?'

'How is she?'

'I'm afraid Rachel's gone into intensive care.'

'What does that mean?' But of course he knew.

'One of her lungs has collapsed and she's on the critical list.' Dad's voice broke. 'Mum and I will have to stay here. Can you fend for yourself for a while?'

'Can't I come over? Where's the hospital?'

There was a long pause.

'I'll ring you later. When we know a little more. It's a bit frantic here. We just wanted to know *you're* all right, at least.'

'Where's Mum?'

'With Rachel.'

As usual, thought Greg, and then was deeply ashamed of himself. Rachel could die and his parents were in terrible distress. Why wasn't he? Rachel was a helpless, innocent baby. What right did he have to – 'Of course I'll be OK here,' said Greg. *I don't care if she busts a gut.* Had he really shouted that at his father? *I don't care if she busts a gut.* It seemed such a long time ago now.

'There's plenty of food in the fridge.'

'I'll manage.'

'Well done, old lad.'

Greg closed his eyes against the 'old lad'. He always hated being called that. His father only used the phrase when he wanted Greg to do something he knew he didn't want to do.

'I'll be fine.'

'We'll keep ringing.'

'OK.'

When his father had rung off, Greg realised he should have said something about Rachel, even if it was only 'good luck'.

He paced about the living room, still in shock, feeling guilty and inadequate. Then his ear began to hurt and Greg went to the mirror, gazing in alarm at how swollen it was.

Greg went into the kitchen, wanting and needing his mother more than he had ever done as a child. He went to the medicine cabinet on the kitchen wall and took out some disprin, put them in a glass, added water and watched them fizz.

When he had drunk his concoction, the pain seemed to ease a little. He switched on the TV, watched a couple of soap operas, and then gradually nodded off to sleep on the sofa.

Greg woke with a headache and a return of the pain in his ear, aware of something he knew he had to deal with. Then Greg realised it was the telephone ringing and got shakily to his feet, stumbling over to pick up the receiver.

'Yes?'

'It's Dad. Where have you been? I've been ringing for ages.'

'I was asleep. I'm sorry. What's the news?'

'They're trying to re-inflate Rachel's lung – but they say she's very poorly.'

'Poorly? What does that mean?'

'It's some damn silly hospital term. But it's not good.'

Greg noticed his hand was shaking so badly that he could hardly hold the receiver. 'I'm thinking of you, Dad. And Mum and Rachel.'

'I know you are. Try and get some more sleep and I'll call you in the morning.'

'What happens if there's – any change?'

'I'll call you in the morning,' said Dad firmly.

Greg went back into the kitchen and looked morosely into the fridge. He didn't feel at all hungry. Then the telephone began to ring again and he stood rigidly in the centre of the room, eventually running back to the phone and grabbing at the receiver, which seemed incredibly slippery, almost falling out of his hands.

'Dad?'

'Er – no. It's Mrs Banks actually. I'm terribly sorry to be phoning so late.'

Greg glanced at the clock on the mantelpiece and saw that it was just after ten pm. He must have slept for longer than he had imagined. 'That's OK.'

'I've already spoken to Sean and Tim.' Mrs Banks sounded agitated.

'Yes?'

'But they haven't seen Ryan. He's mentioned your name several times, and I got your number through Directory Enquiries. Of course you may not even know Ryan. You might not –'

'He's a friend of mine.'

'Have you seen him?' she asked sharply.

'This afternoon.'

'I mean tonight –'

'No.'

'He goes to table tennis on a Sunday but he should have been home for his supper a couple of hours ago. I've tried everywhere.'

Greg's mind raced, knowing at once where Ryan might be. Why hadn't Tim or Sean sussed that out? Or were they simply too afraid? He had to stop them all getting into trouble.

Greg swallowed. He daren't explain about the rink – it would just lead to more trouble at this stage. He had to try and sort it out himself. 'Look – he could be with some – other friends.'

'Why hasn't he phoned me?'

'They're probably out and about. I could try and find them.'

'Would you?' She seemed overjoyed. 'He *always* rings me if he's going to be late. Ryan's usually such a thoughtful boy. Tell him to ring me straightaway.'

'OK,' said Greg, feeling both irresponsible and utterly inadequate.

Greg cycled stiffly down the arterial road to the abandoned roller-skating rink, full of mounting fear and trepidation, sure that Oliver had finally lost control.

There wasn't much traffic on the road, only the occasional powerful headlights of a truck and just a few cars, driving at speed. The night was warm but not too hot and there was a light breeze. Slowly, Greg's muscles became less stiff and soon he was pedalling fast.

Again and again the terrible thoughts blazed across his mind. Oliver was mad. His hatred for Ryan all-consuming, like it was eating him. Oliver was mad, bad and dangerous to know. Where had he heard that before? Gradually the phrase became a rhythm, pounding in his mind until Greg almost felt he was cycling to its beat. Mad, bad and dangerous to know. Mad, bad and –

He almost overshot The Bantam and had to brake hard, skidding to a halt outside the derelict old pub.

Greg got off his bike, pushing it cautiously over the debris-strewn, pot-holed road, down to the rink.

FIFTEEN

Would he be able to get in through the trap door, Greg wondered, or could it only be opened from inside? He then remembered that he had forgotten to bring a torch and cursed himself for being a careless idiot.

Cautiously checking around him, Greg continued to push his bike beside the long, low bulk of the rink until he came to the car park and the wall where he remembered the trap door had been.

Concealing his bike behind some overhanging foliage, Greg knelt down, finding a latch and pulling hard, breaking a couple of fingernails in the process.

Now something was moving, making a terrible creaking sound, and Greg almost dropped the latch in alarm. Slowly, however, he managed to lever it up until it was resting against the scarred concrete wall. A pit yawned below.

Once at the foot of the stairs, Greg found himself standing in pitch darkness. Could he remember the way? With much blundering about, he eventually managed to find an open door and a passage that led to some stairs.

As Greg's eyes became more used to the dark he began to climb until he arrived in another corridor that was vaguely familiar, slightly illuminated by moonlight from a window that faced the car park.

Greg opened yet another door and found himself in the old rink again, shrouded in a dim greyness. Crossing the rink he entered the gym and saw the assault course stretching out before him, a tangle of shapes that were hardly definable.

Greg could just make out another door on the right and he made his way slowly towards it, trying to make as little noise as possible but only succeeding in hitting the tyre tunnel, setting it in scuffling motion. He froze and listened, but there was no sign of anyone coming.

Then Greg kicked something metallic on the floor which rolled and rattled away into the darkness. He searched for some time, eventually grasping something long and rubbery which turned out to be a large torch.

Greg felt a surge of relief, switching it on and discovering the torch had a powerful beam.

Pushing the door open, Greg stepped inside, hearing a low grunting sound. He paused, listening intently. Then he saw Ryan gently swinging.

Ryan was suspended upside down from a platform near the ceiling, high above the ground, with a gag in his mouth, his arms tied behind his back. Dark blood had run to his face and was also caked in his nostrils. The grunting continued and then became more desperate as their eyes locked.

'I'll get you down,' gasped Greg.

He untied Ryan's arms, scrambled up the rope ladder to the platform, found the knot around Ryan's ankles and was just about to untie the cord when he realised that, if he succeeded, Ryan would hit the floor head–first.

Greg knelt down on the platform. 'Listen, Ryan. I'm going to untie the cord and grab your ankles. Then I'll slowly lower you down. Get me?'

There was a grunted reply and a choking, retching sound.

Gradually the cord came loose, and Greg slowly lowered Ryan to the ground. He lay there for a while on his front, working at the gag, eventually pulling it off and then rolling on to his back, panting and gasping, the nosebleed beginning again.

Greg hurried down from the platform and stood over Ryan, holding his nose until the bleeding stopped.

Ryan didn't move, but his breathing gradually began to improve. 'I thought I was going to die. How did you know where I was?'

Slowly, Greg began to explain.

Ryan was sitting up now, looking better, the dark blood in his face draining away. 'I was down at the table tennis club and Pug showed up.'

'Where were Sean and Tim?'

'They don't play. Pug had the other prats with him, but Oliver wasn't there. Anyway, they said my kid sister had fallen off her bike outside.'

'Where is this club?'

'Not far from here. Isn't this where *you* came?' he asked accusingly. 'I saw the assault course. You might have told me where the Geeks hung out. I would have been warned.'

'I'm sorry.'

'So I got outside the club, they grabbed me and Pug put me in a half-nelson. The pain was hell. Then they bundled me across the road and down here.'

'Didn't anyone try and help you?'

'Members of the public?' Ryan gave a throaty, choking laugh. 'They're not likely to approach a gang of boys, are they? Whatever's happening.'

Greg had to agree that he was right. 'So they strung you up.'

'Funny Oliver wasn't around,' said Ryan.

'Maybe they chucked him out after what happened in the park. Or maybe his dad wouldn't let him go out.'

'I still think it's odd.' Ryan was uneasy.

'Can you walk?' asked Greg, not wanting to try and think it all through now.

'Sure.'

'I've got my bike,' Greg said. 'I can take you on the pillion.'

'We should get the hell out of here,' said Ryan. 'Like now.' He grabbed Greg's forearm. 'Thanks for coming. You're a real mate.'

'I found this torch.'

They stared at each other.

'That's weird,' said Ryan slowly. 'That's very weird.'

'One of them must have dropped it,' gabbled Greg, suddenly going cold.

'It's too big to drop.' Ryan was getting very anxious. 'You don't suppose –'

With an hypnotic feeling of doom, Greg watched the door slowly open. He nodded miserably. Ryan had been right. They'd been tricked. It wasn't over. The Big Drop was only just beginning.

Oliver stood in the doorway, another powerful torch in his hand. He looked incredibly bizarre, dressed in a para-military jacket and trousers with a webbing belt in which he had stuck a knife. His head was shaved.

Gathered behind Oliver were the rest of the Geeks, fidgeting nervously.

'What the hell have you done to yourself?' Greg whispered.

'It didn't take long,' replied Oliver with a bright fixed smile.

He walked slowly towards them, followed by Pug, Hassan, Fabian and Denny. Then he pulled the knife out of his belt and the long blade glinted in the torchlight.

'We don't want to play any more games,' said Greg, the shock waves coursing through him. However weirdly Oliver had got himself up, it was his eyes that were the most terrifying. He was staring straight ahead and they were not only very wide, but completely without expression.

'I'm not playing games,' said Oliver in a monotone. 'Why should I want to play games?' He advanced on them again, signalling Pug and Denny who grabbed Greg, and Hassan and Fabian who held Ryan.

Neither of them put up any resistance for there seemed little point in antagonising Oliver any further.

The Geeks dragged the all too familiar cord from their pockets and bound Greg and Ryan securely.

Then Oliver scaled the rope ladder and stood on the platform, picking up a coiled rope and fastening it into a noose. 'Greg gets the Drop,' Oliver shouted down. 'But Ryan gets the big one.' He caressed the noose and then scratched at his shaven head. Suddenly he grinned.

Pug isn't grinning, thought Greg, his mind reeling. Neither were the rest of the Geeks.

How serious *was* Oliver? Or how seriously crazy?

'You'll be dangled by the legs in the usual way,' Oliver explained to Greg gently, almost apologetically.

'Why?'

'You need a lesson.'

'And me?' asked Ryan quietly.

'You're to be hung by the neck until you're dead.' Oliver's voice was normal, steady, even matter-of-fact. Then he turned to Pug. 'Don't worry. It's only my joke.'

'He's not joking!' Greg bellowed, beginning to struggle fiercely. 'You've got to stop him.'

'Oh dear,' said Oliver. 'I think Greg's lost his sense of humour.'

A few minutes later, Greg was hanging upside down, his feet secured by strong cord to the platform. The blood rushed to his head as he dangled there, filling him with a drumming pain as he gazed down at the hard unyielding ground below. He was conscious of Ryan standing on the platform above, but Greg couldn't see him. All he could do was to feel his fear, know how terrified he was, understand his despair.

Could either of them still see this as a joke – a joke that would be called off any moment? Greg didn't think so. He was now sure that it had never been a joke, simply part of an unhinged campaign that he had made worse – for both Oliver *and* Ryan.

'The noose is ready,' said Oliver quietly.

'OK. Joke over.' Ryan's voice was only just above a whisper. 'This is getting dangerous.'

Oliver laughed. 'Everything in life is dangerous.'

'It's not fair.' There was a sob in Ryan's voice now and then he began to plead. 'Just let me go. I'm sorry if I've upset you, Oliver. I'm sorry I bullied you. Look – I'll give you my new bike if you let me go.'

Ryan sounded piteous, a child wanting a game to end,

just as Oliver was a child waiting for a game to start.

Greg felt sick as he swung gently, sure that his eyes were bulging out of their sockets.

'Let him go, Oliver,' he gasped. 'Can't you see he doesn't enjoy the joke? Neither do I.' Greg used the word 'joke' advisedly, but he still prayed that in the final analysis Oliver wouldn't go the full stretch. Then Greg almost laughed hysterically at his unintentional pun.

'Who said either of you were meant to be enjoying the joke?' asked Oliver mildly. 'Besides, it's not a joke at all. Did you ever think it was?'

'I'm just going to slip your head into the noose, Ryan, and then all I have to do is kick your legs off the platform. I think I've got the position right.' Oliver sounded conscientious, trying to do a difficult job well.

Ryan began to plead again. 'I'll give you forty pounds. It's what I've got saved up. You can have it if you let me go. I promise you can have it.' His voice rose shrilly.

'This has got to stop,' bellowed Greg. 'Stop now.'

But Oliver only laughed.

Then, to everyone's surprise, Pug intervened. 'Let him go!'

'No chance,' said Oliver.

'I'm coming to get you off that platform.'

'So are we,' said Hassan.

'Leave them alone,' yelled Denny.

'And they'll come home,' laughed Oliver in childish, mad glee. 'Bringing their tails behind them.'

'You're going too far, Ollie,' shouted Fabian, attempting intimacy. 'Pug's right. The joke's got to be over.'

'Shut up, all of you.' Oliver was contemptuous. 'Ryan needs to be punished most of all.'

'Why?' demanded Ryan.

'Don't you remember?' Oliver's voice was bitter. 'You grabbed my pendant and flushed it down the toilet.'

'It was only a joke,' pleaded Ryan.

'Some joke,' said Oliver. 'My mother gave me that pendant. She gave it to me when she died. It was *her* pendant. And *you* flushed it down the toilet. I'll never see that pendant again. Never.' His voice broke.

'I'm sorry,' whispered Ryan. 'I'm really sorry.'

Greg still had no idea how serious Oliver was. But suppose it was for real? His stomach heaved.

'I'm coming up,' said Pug.

'If you do, I'll kick Ryan's legs away.'

Greg, still swinging, his head pounding, had a flash of optimism. If the Geeks were going to fall out, there was hope for him and Ryan. Or was there?

'Let him down.' Fabian spoke slowly and quietly. 'You're going over the top.'

'No. Ryan is going to do that,' giggled Oliver.

'We're serious,' said Pug. 'Do what we tell you.'

'Why did you let him fix up this noose in the first place?'

demanded Ryan in a desperate return to control.

'We didn't know he'd done it,' said Pug. 'Look, Ollie – knock it off now.'

'Yes,' said Fabian. 'This is getting out of order.'

But Oliver only tightened the noose round Ryan's neck.

'Oliver,' said Greg, exerting every effort to speak calmly and rationally. 'We can sort this out. Talk it over. Can't we?'

'No.' Oliver sounded very certain. 'It's too late for that.'

'Why too late?'

He didn't reply.

'You've got to tell me what's happened.' Then Greg suddenly realised something. Why hadn't he gagged Ryan like he had gagged Sean and Tim? Did he *want* him to talk? Of course he did. Oliver didn't want Ryan silent. He wanted him begging, pleading for his life.

'Where're you going, Pug?' asked Fabian suddenly.

'Home. I'm not putting up with this any longer. I don't want to be involved.'

'You can't rat out now,' yelled Denny.

'We'll be accessories to – murder.' Pug sounded as if he could hardly believe what he was saying.

'You can't just leave us here,' yelled Greg.

'Pug – look –' Hassan began.

'We'll get nicked,' Pug warned them.

'Not if you stop him –' Greg was desperate now.

'He's got a knife,' said Fabian. 'And he's gone crazy. He could kill us all.'

'What about me and Greg?' Ryan was crying now, with great hard, gulping sobs. It was a horrible noise and made Greg even more terrified. Everything and everyone was out of control and soon they could be left alone with Oliver.

'Let's go,' said Pug. 'Let's go now.' He hurried towards the door and the other Geeks followed.

Now we *are* alone with Oliver, thought Greg, and he knew he had to try to reason with him. Ryan's sobs filled the dark and immensely claustrophobic space.

'Let me go,' said Greg. 'It'll be all right. You've got the knife. We can't hurt –'

'You haven't been punished enough, Greg,' said Oliver quietly.

'We can talk.'

'What about?'

Greg desperately searched for a topic. 'What about your *Dream Stealer* then?'

'What about it?'

'If you hurt Ryan, you'll never be able to write with your dad.'

'Why not?' asked Oliver mockingly.

'You'll be put away.'

'I won't be writing any *Dream Stealers*.'

'You won't?'

'I asked my dad tonight.'

'Well?'

'And he said no.'

Another push over the edge, thought Greg. Didn't Adam Anlott have the slightest awareness of his son's mental state? Was he so wrapped up in himself and his writing that he hadn't even noticed?

'Do you love your dad?' asked Greg, determined not to give up, but the slow swinging on the rope was making his head feel as if a hammer was pounding inside his brain. The blood felt heavy, as if it was searching for a place to break out.

'He's my father.'

'Do you want him to respect you?'

'I want him to notice me,' Oliver replied, suddenly sounding perfectly reasonable. 'That's all.' He spoke sadly. 'Maybe he will after this. I mean – I've got to do something, haven't I? I've *got* to get him to notice me.'

'We need to talk. Let me down.' Renewed hope flooded into Greg's pounding mind. Was there a chance?

'We've got nothing more to say, Greg. Not now.'

'We're friends.'

'Correction. We could have been friends. But you lied to me.'

'Oliver –' yelled Greg. Then they both heard the sound of sirens.

'They're not coming here. Don't worry.' Oliver sounded reassuring.

'They might be,' replied Greg.

Oliver was silent for a long time as the sirens came nearer. Then he said, 'The bloody little shit –'

'What are you on about?'

'Pug.'

'What about him?'

'He's called the police.' Oliver spat on the floor of the platform, rage suddenly consuming him.

'How could they get here so fast?' Greg felt a glimmer of hope.

'He's got a mobile, hasn't he?'

'Has he?'

'He nicked one yesterday. He's called the police.' Oliver repeated the statement incredulously.

'Then let me down fast.'

'All right.' Oliver meekly began to untie the rope, and Greg felt a sudden, glorious surge of hope. Ryan was still sobbing.

'You'll have to lower me down,' shouted Greg in sudden panic. 'If you don't I'll hit my head.'

To his immense relief, he felt Oliver's strong hands grip his ankles and slowly, gently, he brought him down.

As Greg staggered to his feet he gasped, 'Now untie my hands.' His head was pounding, nausea welling, but the relief, the gloriously wonderful relief, overcame everything.

'No way.'

'The police will be in here soon.'

'They'll take a bit of time finding their way in.'

'What will they say when they find me with my hands tied behind my back?' demanded Greg.

'I'll tell them it's a game,' said Oliver slowly. 'Just a game.'

'And Ryan?'

Oliver's meekness vanished and the authority returned. 'He's going to have an accident. Accidents do happen in some games, don't they?'

Greg watched him, his heart hammering so painfully that he thought that any moment now he would stop breathing. He felt frozen inside. His will power had hardened over.

'You *are* playing a game,' he said like a child.

'I never play games.' Oliver laughed again. He was standing just behind Ryan who didn't move, seemingly hardly able to believe what was happening. His shoulders were shaking.

The police sirens were louder now.

Oliver was fiddling with the noose.

Then there was a distant crash and the pounding of feet. The door was suddenly kicked open and a flashlight blinded them all.

There was a scream and Ryan fell from the platform, his wrists still tied together.

★

Ryan was lying face down on the floor. He wasn't moving. He didn't make a sound.

Oliver must have unhooked the noose, Greg thought. But did he push him off the platform or had he fallen in his panic and confusion?

One of the police officers ran forward and bent over Ryan.

'What's going on?' he asked, gazing around in bewilderment.

'Just a game,' said Oliver as he hurriedly unbound Greg's wrists.

'What are you up to?'

'We're playing prisoners.'

Half a dozen police officers now filled the room, all with torches, one with a German shepherd dog on a lead, that was beginning to growl threateningly.

The first police officer to arrive was kneeling beside Ryan, checking his pulse. 'He's alive.' The officer looked down at Ryan's leg which was twisted beneath him. Then he felt his neck and Ryan gave a groan. 'Call the paramedics,' he said. 'I think he's broken his leg and his collarbone.' He looked up at Oliver. 'You call this a game?'

Oliver and Greg gazed at each other as if they had just met, as if they were strangers.

'You'd better come down to the station,' said the officer to Oliver and Greg. 'We'll need to ask you some questions, and you'll both have to make statements. This looks like a very serious business to me.'

'It was,' said Oliver calmly. 'It's over now.'

'No, it's not,' replied the officer. 'Not by a long way.'

SIXTEEN

The time was just after three am as Oliver and Greg sat in the back of the police car and glided through the night streets towards Oliver's house, the radio crackling intermittently, the two officers in the front silent, not attempting to communicate with them. Ryan, who had lapsed in and out of consciousness, had been taken to hospital hours ago.

Because Greg had told the police about Rachel and because Oliver's father couldn't be raised by phone, they had both made statements with a social worker present, and were being driven home.

'Dad won't get up at this hour,' Oliver stated miserably. 'Can I come and stay with you, Greg?' He seemed shrunken now, thinner, absurd-looking in his para-military clothes as if they had come from a dressing-up box, and his shaven head looked ridiculously vulnerable.

'You can't. My sister's ill.'

'I didn't know you had one. I thought you were an only child, like me.'

Greg was silent. Was Oliver going to accuse him of lying again?

But he seemed to have gone off on another tack. 'Dad's going to be furious.'

'That's the least of your problems,' said Greg.

'I didn't mean any harm.'

Greg's ear was throbbing badly again and he still had a blinding headache.

'I told you I'm sorry. I lost my temper.'

'That's not all you lost.'

'What do you mean?'

'You lost your marbles. You need help.' Greg was detached and purposeful.

'Whose?'

'I don't know.' He wasn't prepared to go any further.

'Will *you* help me?' Oliver asked sadly.

'How?' Greg was wary.

'We could be friends. You could meet my dad.'

'I don't want to.'

'Be friends?'

'Meet your dad.'

'Why not?' Oliver sounded as if one of his trump cards had suddenly been abruptly removed. 'He's famous. Don't you want to meet a famous person?'

'I'd rather have met your mum,' said Greg suddenly. 'She sounded quite something.'

'She was.' For the first time Oliver seemed sincere. 'You know –' He paused.

'What?'

Oliver shook his head.

'I'm sorry,' Greg said inadequately.

★

The police officer walked up the drive with Oliver and Greg. He had only allowed Greg to join them because Oliver had become hysterical, and his colleague was only a few steps behind them ready to take Greg back to the car again.

The house was in darkness, but Oliver babbled on without seeming to realise what had happened, who he was with or what was going to happen. He seemed completely spaced out.

'Please come and meet my dad.'

'*Now?*'

'Why not?'

'You crazy or something?' The irony didn't escape Greg and he suddenly felt a rush of pity for Oliver. 'You scared?'

'What am I going to say to him?' Oliver was childishly inept, wanting advice, wanting to depend on him.

'Has he seen the way you look?' asked Greg.

'No.'

'Then he's going to go ballistic, isn't he?'

'He might not. If *you* say something.'

'But what?' Greg hissed. 'What the hell can I say? It's quarter past three in the morning, you've shaved your head, you look like Action Man – and – where's that knife?' He couldn't think how he could possibly have forgotten about Oliver's weapon.

'What knife?' asked the police officer, uneasily. He seemed really worried and kept darting glances at Oliver as he continued talking feverishly.

'I threw it away.'

'We'll pick it up later.'

'Good,' said Oliver. 'You don't want to leave it lying around, do you? It could hurt someone.'

The officer didn't reply.

Oliver rang the bell again and again while Greg and the police officer stood on either side of him.

Eventually they heard footsteps and the front door slowly opened on a chain.

'Well?' asked the dark bearded figure.

'It's me, Dad,' began Oliver, but the officer cut in.

'I'm sorry, Mr Cole. You son was involved in an incident. I need to talk to you about him. We tried to ring you before, but there was no reply.'

The chain came off and the door opened wide as Adam Anlott stood there in his dressing gown, staring down at his son in amazement.

'What have you done to yourself?' His voice was neutral, and he didn't sound as if he cared in the slightest what Oliver had done to himself.

'It was part of the game,' faltered Oliver. Then he suddenly began to cry, not with great harsh gulping sobs like Ryan had, but with the tears pouring down his face, silently weeping.

His father made no attempt to comfort him.

'Are you Oliver's friend?' asked Adam Anlott at last, turning to Greg in frustration.

He didn't hesitate. 'Yes.'

'What have you both done?'

'I'll talk to you about that, sir,' said the police officer. 'Can we come in?'

'There's no one here.'

It was a curious statement and it began to repeat itself in Greg's exhausted mind. *There's no one here. There's no one here. There's no one —*

'I'll call you tomorrow,' said Greg awkwardly.

'I hope your sister gets better.' Oliver suddenly and surprisingly sounded completely normal.

Greg turned away and began to walk back down the drive. The police officer fell in step beside him. He heard the front door slam. He knew he'd have to come back. Someone had to.

Greg checked the telephone answering machine and to his immense relief there was no message. Suddenly he was ravenously hungry, and going to the fridge pulled out cheese and ham and corned beef, placing a slice of each between slices of white bread. As he ate, Greg remembered Oliver's corned-beef hash, the dish that he had so much enjoyed, the lovingly prepared dish that Adam Anlott had so cruelly rejected.

After eating his fill and drinking a can of coke, Greg went

back into the sitting room and lay down on the sofa. But sleep wouldn't come so he switched on the television and began to watch a movie. Five minutes later his eyes began to close.

Greg was woken by the shrilling of the phone and levered himself up, shambling across the carpet as early morning sunlight filtered the room with a golden haze, and he remembered he had forgotten to draw the curtains.

'Did I wake you?'

'No, Dad,' he lied.

'Rachel's got through the night which is a good sign, but we don't know whether she's going to make it or not.'

There was a long silence.

'How's Mum?' Greg asked eventually.

'We want you here with us. I'm sorry about last night. I was in such a state. I'm coming home to pick you up,' said Dad. 'We should all be together. Have a hot drink. I'll be back in half an hour.'

Greg lay down again on the sofa, his shoulders heaving, and as he wept he imagined Oliver and Ryan weeping too. It was as if they were all three crying together.

'There she is, old boy.' His father gazed down at Rachel who was lying in a cot in a side ward.

Greg's mother was sitting beside her, exhausted, looking up at him like a child herself.

Rachel seemed minute and her face was a strange and frightening mauve colour. Her eyes were closed and she was breathing in short, shallow gasps.

'Is she going to be all right?' Greg asked, not exactly addressing the question to either of them.

Dad answered too quickly. 'We don't know yet. She's making a fight of it.'

Greg exchanged a glance with his mother, knowing how afraid she was and how desperately she needed reassurance.

Rachel whimpered huskily but didn't open her eyes.

'We should pray for her,' Greg half whispered, aware he hadn't prayed in years.

His mother nodded eagerly.

Dad cleared his throat.

There was a silence between them, but it was the silence of companionship, not apartness.

Rachel gurgled slightly.

Soon, either way, Greg knew that they would all have a lot to tell each other.

Please, God, let her live, he said to himself inside. There was a lot of living to do. He needed Rachel to be part of that living. They all did. They would all be together.